To

J

Fairy Rescuers

Return to Elysia

Enjoy the adventure

Karen Cogan

Fairy Rescuers

Return to Elysia

Karen Langtree

© Karen Langtree, 2012

Published by OneWay Press

Reprinted 2014

ISBN 978-0-9561086-6-1

Illustrations by Josh Atkinson

Book design by Clare Brayshaw

Prepared and printed by:

York Publishing Services Ltd
64 Hallfield Road
Layerthorpe
York YO31 7ZQ
Tel: 01904 431213

Website: www.yps-publishing.co.uk

Thank you Thank you Thank you

To:

My editors at OneWay Press: Olive Overton and Ian Smith, who have painstakingly read the manuscript many times and helped me to see what I couldn't see for looking!

The group of children from Burton Green Primary School in York who have helped me by reading and commenting on the manuscript. A very valuable perspective.

Josh – the fabulous illustrator who has done such a wonderful job on this book. What a find you were!

YPS for advice, prompt service and great production.

All the children who have said to me: 'Please write another book about Ellie and Lucy!'

Here it is...

About the Author

Karen is the author of the very popular, My Wicked Stepmother, as well as the previous book in this series: Fairy Rescuers. She lives in York with her husband and two children. Sadly, they now only have one naughty guinea pig!

Karen has loved to write since she was a child, creating songs, stories and musicals. She has a passion to see children discover the wonderful world of story! She visits schools, doing workshops in song-writing and story-writing, as well as working part time as a teacher, in a York primary school. She has a degree in English, drama and philosophy.

When she is an old lady, Karen would like to live in a cottage by the surging sea, in beautiful Northumberland. Every day she will walk her imaginary dog (who will be able to change into any kind of dog, whenever Karen wants him to) along the beach every day. Perfect!

Karen loves to hear from her readers, and replies to every email.

You can contact Karen via her website www.karenlangtree.com or email her at info@onewaypress.co.uk

About the Illustrator

Josh Atkinson is a recent first honours graduate from the city of York. In a short time Josh has been able to become a successful illustrator and also an upcoming award-winning author through the work he has done on children's books for the iPad. His core focus is vector illustration and character design though he also likes to dabble in the area of graphic design. He hopes to one day blur the line between digital storytelling and interactivity so that children of all ages can not only read books but also take part in the story itself.

You can contact Josh via his blog

www.venomousslugdesigns.co.uk

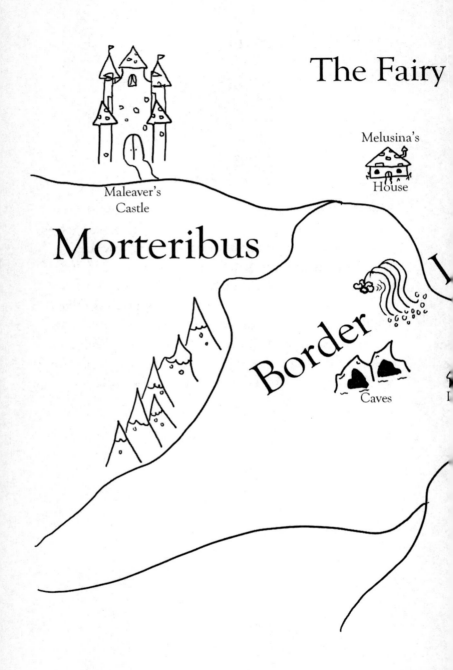

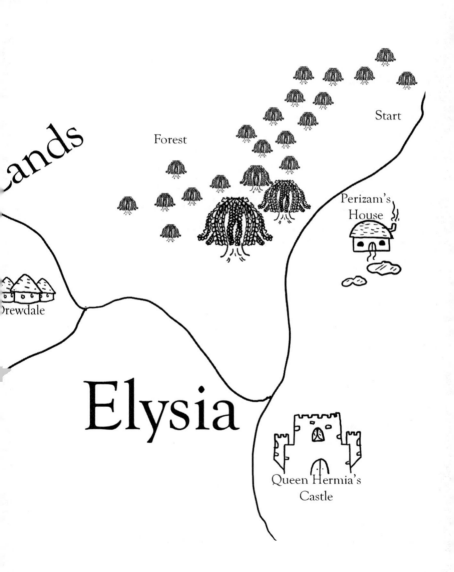

World

Forest

Start

ands

Perizam's
House

Drewdale

Elysia

Queen Hermia's
Castle

Prologue

Gabriella drew her knees up to her chest and hunched her shoulders, bringing her wings around her for comfort. From her window seat, high up in the tower room, she could see into the courtyard and beyond, across the countryside. A mist swirled over the grey-green fields under a constantly gloomy sky. The courtyard was a bustle of activity: Horses were being moved to and from the stables, servants appeared and disappeared through doors, chickens squawked and flew up into the air as dogs chased them. It could have made her smile or even laugh under different circumstances. She remembered the last time she was here... and shuddered.

Across the room, lying on a long couch, watching her, was the boy. She didn't have to look at him to know that he was watching her – she could feel his eyes trained on her like two sentries on duty. Every so often he would speak to her (more like growl at her) and try to make her look at him, but she ignored him, hoping he would give up. He was very like his father in looks – a flash of black hair, dark pools for eyes, a handsome face. But he also had his father's way of speaking; proudly, with a sneer, expecting to be obeyed. Gabriella wondered how long Maleaver's son would allow her to ignore him before he lost his temper.

'Just accept it, Princess. My father brought you here to marry me. There is no way to escape.'

Gabriella did not reply. She knew very well what Maleaver meant to do with her. He thought that by marrying her to his son he could cement his claim on the kingdom of Elysia. She feared for her parents, Queen Hermia and Prince Lysander. What plans did he have for them once she was married to his son? She shivered. The boy noticed.

'Are you cold *dear* Princess?' he sneered. 'Well you'd better get used to it. My father likes things cold, dark and gloomy.'

At that moment a key grated in the lock of the heavy oak door. Gabriella turned to see who would enter. Maleaver strode into the room, his tall dark figure loomed over the boy.

'Well?' he demanded of his son.

'She still refuses to speak to me, Father,' the boy replied, sulkily. 'I'm bored of her company. I wish to go and practise my archery.'

Maleaver replied with the back of his hand across the boy's face. 'You will stay here until she speaks to you.' He strode across the room to Gabriella and turned her face to his. 'You foolish little fairy. Make life easier for yourself. Speak to Lucan. He is to be your husband soon so you might as well get to know him.' He thrust Gabriella away from him and stormed back towards the door. 'Useless boy!' he muttered as he swept out of the room, locking the door behind him.

Lucan put his hand up to his reddened cheek. He narrowed his eyes at Gabriella, like a cornered cat, then abruptly turned his back on her.

Gabriella closed her eyes. 'Help will come,' she told herself. 'Help *will* come.'

Chapter One

Help!

'Hey Lucy, you did really well tonight!' Ellie said, as they walked out to the car park to meet Lucy's dad, after Karate.

'Thanks,' Lucy said, Ellie's compliment making her grin. 'I still can't believe my mum finally gave in and let me do Karate. I love it.'

'Your dad was a big help,' Ellie reminded her. 'There he is.' She pointed across the car park as Mr. Pennington got out of his car, waving at them. They ran towards him and got in.

'Good session?' he asked.

'Yeah, really good. Lucy's brilliant,' Ellie said. 'The Sensei says she will be able to go for her blue belt soon.'

'Great!' Lucy's dad said.

Lucy turned to Ellie in the back of the car and whispered, 'It seems such a long time since this all started with our adventure in Elysia,' she sighed.

Ellie glanced at Mr. Pennington but he was singing along to some rock music on the radio. 'I sometimes wonder if I dreamed it, you know. But then, we probably wouldn't be friends if I had.'

Mr. Pennington dropped Ellie at her door. 'See you at school tomorrow Lucy,' she said. 'And thanks for the lift Mr. P.'

'No problem Ellie.'

'Hi Mum!' Ellie shouted, heading for the kitchen. Mrs. Deaver was at the table, tapping away on her laptop. 'Hi Mum!' Ellie shouted again, jumping around in front of her mother and waving exaggeratedly.

'Oh, hi love,' Mrs. Deaver said, finally looking up from some lesson plan or other. 'Good session?'

'Yeah, great.'

'How's Lucy doing?'

'Fab!'

'Excellent. I've just got to finish this...' Mrs. Deaver was sucked back in by her computer screen.

Ellie rummaged in the cupboard to find the biscuit barrel. Her four year old brother Callum came into the kitchen. Seeing Ellie munching biscuits, he wanted one too.

'Give me a sbickit Ellie,' Callum said.

'What do you say?' Ellie asked, holding the barrel out of his reach.

'Give me a sbickit!' he repeated, jumping up to grab the barrel out of Ellie's hand.

'Not 'til you say the magic word,' Ellie teased.

'I want a sbickit!' Callum shouted and began to pull on Ellie's arm.

'Oh Ellie,' said Mum, looking up, irritated, from her computer. 'Just give him one!'

He hasn't said the magic word,' Ellie said.

'No such thing as magic!' Callum shouted.

'That's what you think!' Ellie said, still holding the biscuit barrel away from him.

'Ellie!' snapped Mrs. Deaver. 'Give him a sbickit... I mean biscuit. And Callum – say PLEASE!'

Ellie headed upstairs to her room. It was strange that Lucy had mentioned their rescue mission in Elysia tonight. Gabriella had been on Ellie's mind over the last few days too, but she always looked sad.

'I wish you could just email or text fairies and find out what they're up to,' she said to herself.

After getting her football kit ready for the practise the next day at school, Ellie watched some TV with Callum (who had now decided that he liked her again). He curled up with his head in her lap and Ellie endured another half an hour of Thomas the Tank Engine before their dad came in and took Callum to bed.

When Ellie woke up the next morning she felt very uncomfortable, as if something had been digging into her face all night. Rubbing her cheek, she lifted her pillow. Something *had* been digging into her: A rock – about the size of a small apple! 'Callum!' she thought, picking up the rock, ready to storm into his room. But as she picked it up, she saw a small piece of paper, folded several times, tied to the rock with thin silvery thread, which wasn't easy to break. The paper, even when opened out, was only about four centimetres square. There was some tiny writing on the paper but it was impossible to read. Ellie knew immediately that it was from Elysia. Her heart began to beat very fast. 'Need a magnifying glass,' she muttered, jumping up from her bed then looking around her messy room in despair. 'Don't have one. Darn. Who will have one?' She thought for a moment. 'Callum! Mum bought him that set, with a magnifying glass, for his bugs.'

She put the little piece of paper under the rock on her desk and marched into Callum's room.

'Can I borrow your magnifying glass Callum?' she asked.

Callum was playing with his trains on the bedroom floor. He looked up at her and raised his eyebrows. 'Magic word?' he said.

'Yes, yes. Ok. PLEASE.'

'Please what?' Callum insisted.

'Please, please, please, please, PLEASE can I borrow your magnifying glass?'

Callum put on his fake posh voice. ''Course you can my sister. It is over there with some bugs.' He pointed to his little desk where several dead bugs lay in margarine tubs.

Ellie picked up the magnifying glass. 'Thank you, very kind little brother,' she said, rubbing his hair as she left the room.

'What do you want it for?' Callum asked, popping his head around the door, suddenly curious.

'Never you mind,' Ellie shouted, slamming her bedroom door behind her. She picked up the paper and held the magnifying glass above it, but her hands were shaking so much she had to put the paper down to be able to read it. It said:

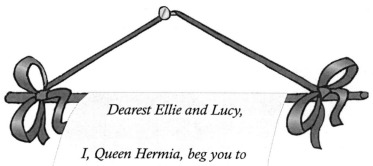

Dearest Ellie and Lucy,

I, Queen Hermia, beg you to come to our aid once again. Gabriella has been kidnapped by Maleaver! Go to Perizam's house and he will tell you more. I send a tube of fairy dust to shrink you. Please come. Gabriella is in grave danger.

THIS MESSAGE IS BROUGHT TO YOU
BY TOOTHFAIRIES INC
PS. SORRY ABOUT THE ROCK!

Ellie's eyes widened. She read the note several times. Where was the fairy dust? She pounced on her pillow and looked underneath it again. About to roll down behind the mattress was a tube, no bigger than Ellie's thumb nail, filled with shimmering purple dust.

'Wow!' Ellie gasped. 'Fairy magic! I didn't know you could bottle this stuff.'

As she dressed, Ellie began to plan. She put the tube and the note into her shirt pocket to show Lucy. She would have to get Lucy to come home with her this afternoon. Then they could stand on the magical pathway, by her shed, like they did before, and get pulled into the Fairy World.

Ellie was excited and nervous at the same time. She was itching to get to school. 'Come on, come on!' she urged her mum and Callum as she stood by the door at quarter to eight. Ellie and Callum had to go to breakfast club, as their mum and dad needed to be at work early. Ellie wanted to make time go faster and wished she had some magic of her own.

'Ellie, we've got ten minutes yet,' Mum said. 'Something special going on today?'

Ellie tried to sound casual. 'No, just want to get to school to see Rhys and Tom. Catch up on some footie stuff, you know.'

'Hmmm,' said Mum, eyeing her suspiciously.

As it was, when everyone was finally ready, Ellie forgot her football kit, in her excitement, and they had to go back for it. 'Now we're going to be late!' moaned Mum.

Of course Ellie knew she wouldn't see Lucy until first break. Lucy never came to breakfast club and she was only in year three, whereas Ellie was in year five. Tom and Rhys were talking about the match their team were playing tomorrow after school. It was against their closest rivals, St. Bartholomew's Primary.

'We'll easily beat them,' Tom was saying, 'especially if Ell's on form. They'll be lucky to score at all!' Ellie had a reputation for being the best under eleven goalie in town.

'Yeah no worries,' Rhys added. 'Right Ell?'

She was staring out of the window. Gabriella's sad face had crossed her mind again – and now she knew why she'd been thinking about her recently.

'Hey aren't you bothered Ell?' Rhys said. He nudged her.

'Hmm? Oh... yeah... 'course I am. St Bart's? We'll wipe the floor with them.'

'You better be up for it Ell,' Tom said.

'I am,' she said.

But in her heart, she knew she had more important things to tackle before that match tomorrow.

'Hey Lucy!' Ellie called across the playground at break time.

Lucy was playing with some of her friends from year three. She looked up and waved as Ellie headed towards her.

'I need to talk to you,' she said, hooking her arm through Lucy's. Lucy always felt important in front of her friends when Ellie Deaver from year five came up to her in the playground. Not only did Ellie have the amazing goal-keeper reputation but she was also the girl who had brought down the bully, Nikki Walters from year six.

'What's up?' Lucy asked, with some concern in her voice, as Ellie hurried her away from her friends.

'We can't talk here. We need somewhere private.' Ellie pulled Lucy round the back of the PE store and crouched down. She looked around as if she were in a spy movie, which would have made Lucy laugh if she hadn't realised that something serious was going on.

'What's wrong?' Lucy repeated, feeling her heart start to beat a little faster.

'Look,' Ellie said, pulling the tiny piece of paper from her pocket, along with the magnifying glass.

Lucy gasped. 'Is it from Gabriella?'

'Not exactly,' Ellie said. 'Read it.' Lucy took the paper from Ellie's hand and applied the magnifying glass. All the while Ellie kept watch around the PE store in case anyone should overhear them.

Lucy was horrified. 'Maleaver has got Gabriella? That's terrible.'

'I know. We need to get there as soon as possible. Are you up for it?'

'Of course,' Lucy said, without hesitation. 'Do you have the fairy dust?'

Ellie brought it out of her pocket. Lucy took it carefully and turned it around in her fingers, admiring the colour as the specks of dust twinkled in the light.

'Can you come to my house after school today?' Ellie said.

'I'd have to go home first and ask my mum, and she'd probably say no 'cos it's Brownies tonight,' Lucy said. 'What if we could find a way there before that? We should go as soon as possible. No one will know we're gone. Time seemed to stand still here last time we were in the Fairy World.'

'Well, not quite,' Ellie said, remembering that a little time had passed in this world last time. 'But I agree. I want to get there NOW if we can. But how?'

'What about the copse?' Lucy suggested. At the bottom of their school field was a small wooded area known as the copse. Children were not supposed to go into it without a teacher. 'We could look for a pathway there at lunch time.'

Ellie smiled at Lucy, who was not normally one to break any rules. 'How would we know? We had Gabriella to feel the magic last time?'

'Maybe we have to use a tiny bit of the dust to feel the magic.'

'Won't that shrink us?' Ellie asked.

'I don't know. Maybe if we just use a little bit it will help us to sense any pull from a Fairy pathway.'

Ellie wasn't sure but she was excited about getting back to Elysia. 'Okay. We'll try it. Meet me here as soon as you've finished your lunch.'

As the two girls stood up, their eyes met the sneering face of Nikki Walters. 'So, Ellie Deaver believes in fairies does she? Making up little stories with your year three friend?'

'Oh get lost, Nikki,' Ellie said.

'Wouldn't your footie pals love to hear about this,' Nikki sniggered.

Ellie felt her cheeks begin to burn, but she knew Nikki was always looking for ways to wind her up since Ellie had made a fool of her. Lucy stepped forward. Her confidence had grown since she had begun Karate with Ellie. She wasn't scared of Nikki anymore. 'Go away Nikki. Ellie is not bothered who you tell. No one would believe you anyway.' Ellie *was* actually bothered, but she wasn't going to show it.

'I heard your little plan for a game in the copse at lunch-time. I might just tell Mrs. White,' Nikki said.

Lucy looked nervously at Ellie. 'Go on then,' Ellie said. 'But if you do, I'll tell her you've been picking on Lucy again. And who do you think she'll believe?' With that, Ellie took Lucy by the arm and walked away, leaving Nikki scowling after them. 'Ignore her Lucy. Stick to the plan. Just keep your eyes peeled for teachers.'

The rest of the morning went painfully slowly. Ellie could not concentrate on fractions and Lucy could not concentrate on the poem she was supposed to be writing. Both girls kept looking at the clock and wishing it would hurry up and reach 12.15.

In the dining hall Ellie wolfed down her food and shot out before Lucy's class had even come in. She kept fingering the little tube of fairy dust in her pocket.

Every time she touched it she felt as if she could hear Gabriella's voice calling her to hurry. Lucy was tempted not to eat much but she knew she would need the energy if they were about to head off on an adventure. Her stomach fluttered with a thousand butterflies.

Nikki was watching her from the year six table.

Lucy and Ellie met by the PE store. 'Are you ready?' Ellie said.

'I think so,' Lucy replied. 'I hope we can find a path. I'm a bit scared too.'

'That's okay, Lucy. So am I. You can't be brave if you're not scared first.' She smiled at Lucy. Then she looked around to see if the coast was clear. There were a couple of dinner ladies milling around the playground. 'Once they turn their backs, make a run for the copse,' Ellie said.

It took them twenty seconds (Ellie was counting) to run panting into the woods and collapse behind a tree.

'Get the fairy dust out,' Lucy said.

Ellie took the tiny tube and very carefully eased the lid off. Some purple dust was already on her fingers. 'How shall we do this?'

Lucy thought for a moment. 'Here.' She took the tube and held it onto the end of her finger, tipping it slightly, then rubbed a streak of purple glittery dust across her forehead. Ellie did the same, then put the lid tightly back onto the tube.

'Let's hope we feel something. Do you remember what it was like last time?' Ellie said.

'Yes it felt like we were little paper clips being attracted by a strong magnet,' Lucy said.

They walked close to every tree and down each little pathway they could see. Ellie heard a crack behind them, like a twig snapping, and turned sharply.

'What's wrong?' Lucy asked.

'Didn't you hear that?' Ellie said.

'There are lots of noises, Ellie. The playground's just over there. You're jumpy already.'

'I know.' Ellie agreed. 'Have you felt anything yet?'

'No, nothing.'

They kept walking, touching trees, exploring paths. Just as they were about to give up, Lucy's hand, which she had rested on a tree, began to tingle. She pulled Ellie's hands onto the tree. 'What?' Ellie asked. Then she felt it too. Both girls looked at each other with wide eyes; their hearts began to pound. They started to walk in different directions from the tree with their fingers outstretched. Ellie felt it: The tingling spread through her fingers and hands, then it was like someone was pulling her arms.

'Lucy – here!'

Lucy ran to the spot and stretched out her arms in the same direction. She felt it too. 'Quick! The dust.' Ellie hastily unscrewed the lid of the tube and sprinkled more dust onto them both. As soon as she did this, the pull of the magical pathway became so strong that Ellie dropped the tube. 'Here we go!' she yelled, grabbing Lucy's hand.

At that moment Nikki Walters jumped out from behind a tree. 'Aha! Caught you playing your little fairy games!' she shouted. But she was soon silenced.

Lucy and Ellie had vanished!

Chapter Two

Meetings

She had heard their voices only a moment ago. She had definitely followed them into the copse. And yet, as she ran this way and that through the trees, there was no sign of them. Where were they hiding? This made her even madder. She went back to the spot where she had last heard their voices. As she stood there, puzzled, she spotted something purple glistening on the ground. Picking it up, she sniggered to herself. This must be the 'fairy dust' she had heard them talking about. Just a little tube of purple glitter. There was not much left, so she sprinkled it into her palm and threw it up in the air. She watched it fall, like a shower of purple rain, onto her head. How she would enjoy ribbing Ellie Deaver about this when she found her and her little 'fairy friend' Lucy. But, as the thought crossed her mind, she suddenly felt as if she was being sucked into a giant vacuum cleaner. She tried to scream. She tried to grab hold of a tree. But before she could save herself, she too disappeared from the copse.

It was another bumpy landing for Ellie and Lucy as they arrived in the fairy world. This time they were on the edge of a wood, near a field by a river. They picked themselves up, rubbing various sore parts of their bodies, and looked around. The light was grey, as if it was early morning. There was a mist hanging over the field and the river. Lucy shivered. It reminded her of the last time they were here and their encounter with the nasty goblin, Grizzle. She looked across the river, half expecting to see his hooded figure in a boat, but there was no one. Ellie shivered too. It was cold. She pulled her hands inside the sleeves of her school sweatshirt.

'Do you think this is the same river as before?' she asked.

'I don't know,' Lucy replied. 'I hope so, because it would make it easier to find Perizam's house. But we could be anywhere. We came on a different path.'

'Maybe we should have waited 'til we got back to my house,' Ellie said. Lucy nodded. Suddenly everything seemed much more frightening.

Ellie sensed Lucy's fear and tried to jolly her along. 'Well, let's choose a direction and follow it. If we don't find Perizam's house after a long time maybe there will be someone we could ask.' She wasn't too convinced of this plan herself, but added. 'Come on Lucy, it will be ok. You'll see.'

Lucy tried to smile. 'Which way then?'

Ellie closed her eyes. She tried to picture Perizam. 'This way,' she decided suddenly, linking her arm through Lucy's and turning left to follow the river.

'Do you recognise anything?' Ellie asked, when they had been following the river for quite some time. The dawn light was turning more yellow now and the sun was beginning to penetrate the mist. Feeling warmer and more positive as they walked together, the two friends had been recalling the first time they had been to Perizam's house.

'It's hard to tell,' Lucy said. 'We could be somewhere in England if we didn't know we had been shrunk and flown to another world.' She giggled. It all sounded so unreal.

'I hope we can help Gabriella,' Ellie said. 'I'm not sure why Queen Hermia needs us. She must have hundreds of fairies and other creatures she could call on. And there's the Prince.'

'But you had some kind of special bond with Gabriella,' Lucy said. 'Don't you remember all the things she said to you? And when Maleaver tried to turn her to stone and you jumped in front of her his magic just bounced off you.'

Ellie was silent. It seemed such a huge responsibility.

'Hey Ellie,' Lucy said. 'Is that a person I can see in the distance?'

Ellie squinted. 'I think so. Bit hard to tell from here with it still being a bit misty. We should be careful; they may not be friendly.'

As the girls drew nearer, the figure began to move towards them.

'They've seen us. Keep calm Lucy and let me do the talking.'

Although their hearts began to race, Lucy and Ellie tried to look like they were just out for a walk by the river. All of a sudden Lucy screeched. 'It's him! It's Perizam!'

Ellie's eyes widened as, moments after Lucy, she had recognised him too. They began to run towards the stocky figure ambling towards them. 'Perizam!' they cried, flinging their arms around the small, old man.

Perizam chuckled as the girls smothered him in kisses and hugs. 'I've been waiting for you,' he said. 'I felt it when you arrived and thought I'd come to meet you.'

'But how did you...' then Lucy remembered that Perizam had a gift of knowledge that had helped them many times during their last adventure.

'Come on. My house is not far now. I caught some trout this morning and I've a pot of holmi warming over the fire.'

Lucy and Ellie smiled at each other and linked their arms one through each of Perizam's. Everything felt much better now.

As soon as they entered the little wooden house Ellie and Lucy remembered it well. It was made up of only one room, with a little kitchen at one end and a cosy sofa in front of the welcoming fire. Perizam's bed was a palette on the floor in another corner. Soon the girls were squashed in front of the fire, eating fish and drinking the sweet woody drink called holmi. It suddenly felt like home, even though it looked nothing like home! After some catching up conversation, it was now time to talk about the reason they had been summoned back to Elysia.

'So, the Queen's note arrived safely and you have responded very quickly,' said Perizam.

'Yes. Please tell us what's happened to Gabriella,' Ellie said.

Perizam folded his hands across his large stomach. 'Maleaver is more determined than ever to have Elysia in his power. His plan this time is to marry the princess to his own son – Lucan, so that he can rule the kingdom through them.'

'Maleaver has a son?' exclaimed Lucy.

'Yes. The boy is only a few years older than the princess. Maleaver sent him away when he was a small child and has recently had him brought back to his castle – to use the boy as part of his plan, I assume.'

'But where is his mother?' Lucy asked.

'The rumour is that she died shortly after giving birth to the boy and that is why Maleaver sent him away. He couldn't bear to look on him.'

'But who was she?' Ellie asked.

'No one really knows. Some unfortunate creature, like Silveria nearly was, I imagine, when Maleaver put her under his spell.'

'So he kidnapped Gabriella. But what about the Queen and Prince? If they are still alive he won't be able to rule Elysia,' Ellie said.

'No. I'm sure he has some scheme to get rid of them too but we don't know it. At the moment the Queen is being heavily guarded in her palace but Prince Lysander is away on business with a Kingdom across the Timeless Sea. He doesn't even know about any of this yet. Messengers have been sent.'

'Oh!' said Lucy. 'This is awful.'

'How are we supposed to help, Perizam?' asked Ellie.

'Well, the Queen dispatched a rescue party as soon as she realised what had happened. There were three of them – the very best. Fychan – a water nymph. An excellent archer. Adalira – a worker of powerful magic through her beautiful lyre playing. And Acantha – a woodland nymph. A great thinker and planner and a master of fairy martial arts.'

'So why does she need us? I don't get it,' Ellie said.

'Unfortunately the rescue party have disappeared. They have stopped contacting the Queen and she is very worried about them,' Perizam continued.

'Are we meant to find them too?' asked Lucy, becoming more anxious at the task set before them.

'Princess Gabriella is the main priority,' Perizam said.

'Are you coming with us?' Lucy asked hopefully.

'Not this time child. I have not been well and besides, I sense that you will gain help and strength along the way. You won't need me,' Perizam said, smiling at Lucy and taking her hands in his.

'But we don't have any magic to help us,' Ellie said.

'You have your own kind of magic, child,' Perizam said. 'Today we will pack a few provisions and think about how you are going to get into Maleaver's castle this time. Then a good night's rest and you can set off early in the morning.'

Minutes after Lucy and Ellie had turned a bend following the river's course, Nikki Walters crash landed in the field. Sitting up, she looked around her at the ordinary looking field and river. She shook her head in confusion wondering where she was and how she could possibly be there. A little knot was forming in her stomach. She looked around for someone to help her, but there was no one. Her eyes began to sting but she balled her fists into them until they stopped.

She stood up and brushed herself down. Taking a deep breath she said aloud, 'I'll just have to go and find some help. There must be a farmhouse or something nearby.'

Ignoring the river, she set off in the opposite direction, looking for a path or track to follow.

By midday she was feeling very hot. The sun was directly overhead and she had walked for miles through several fields, along a track and over a bridge. She had seen no one at all and come across only one building – an abandoned farm house. She was beginning to feel anxious that she would never get back home or see another living being again. To top it all, she was hungry, very thirsty and very very grumpy.

She sat down on a boulder by the side of the track. For a few moments she closed her eyes to think. Pictures of her mum pressed into her mind and she felt her eyes begin to sting again. She blinked hard, stood up and looked around. Across the field, to her left, was a wood and she thought she saw a thin wisp of smoke rising out of the trees. She squinted and shielded her eyes from the sun. Yes, it was real. 'There must be someone there making the fire,' she thought, so she set off across the field to find out.

In the wood she came across a small dwelling. It couldn't really be called a house. It had been put together with sticks, moss and leaves, and served as a shelter from the weather. It was only high enough for one – maybe two people to crouch inside. As Nikki approached cautiously from behind, she saw a small figure, draped in a cloak, with its back to her. The figure was toasting something on a long stick, over a fire, and singing to itself in a tuneless whining voice. It was small enough to be a child and certainly smaller than Nikki. Whatever it was toasting smelled very good. She marched up to the creature.

Hearing branches crunching, it turned round, looking at Nikki with large startled eyes. Nikki too was taken aback because this was not a child – in fact, it was not something that she had ever seen before in her life. The creature had pale grey skin and very large pointed ears that stuck out at right angles under the hood of its cloak. Its lips were thin and its arms and legs spindly. Nikki took a step backwards from the ugly creature.

'What do you want?' demanded the creature, eyeing her suspiciously.

'I... I... I'm hungry and thirsty,' Nikki stammered.

The creature laughed. 'So am I. Go and find your own food.' He waved Nikki away and turned back to his fire.

Nikki came closer. 'I need a drink of water at least.'

'Go find a stream then,' the creature said, without even looking up at her.

Nikki looked at the fish he was holding over the fire. It smelt so good. Her stomach began to growl. 'Hey, stop being so mean and give me a bit of your food. I'm lost and I don't know when I'll find anything else. Everything round here is so weird and...'

The creature looked up suddenly, poking a long bony finger at her. 'You're human aren't you?' he said slowly.

'Yes, of course I'm human. What else would I be?'

The creature sniggered. 'Never been here before have you?'

'No, I doubt it or I wouldn't be lost, would I?' Nikki

said, placing her hands on her hips. She was really starting to dislike this little whatever-it-was.

'How did you get here?' asked the creature.

'Give me some food and I'll tell you,' Nikki said.

The creature looked at his fish. Drool was dripping from his lips. He licked them with a long slimy tongue and considered. Nikki pulled a disgusted face.

'Sit,' he ordered and gestured to Nikki to sit on a log opposite the fire.

She did as she was told. The creature removed the fish from the heat and took another stick that had been sharpened at the end. He speared the fish with it and pulled it into two pieces. He gave the smaller piece to Nikki on the end of the stick.

She took a bite, hungrily, but had to spit it out quickly.

'Hot, human. Wait.'

The creature proceeded to eat his piece without any trouble. Gradually the fish cooled and Nikki ate it in three mouthfuls. She would never have eaten fish at home, but she was too hungry to care what it was.

'Can I have some water?' Nikki said. 'You must have some. Please.'

'It says 'pleeeeese,' now,' the creature mimicked. He passed Nikki a can of water. She drank greedily, some of the water dripping down the front of her school uniform.

The creature watched her. 'So, how did you get here?'

'I don't know. One minute I was in the copse at school, spying on these two girls playing stupid fairy games: The next, I was flying through the air and landing in a field miles away from anywhere. Then I walked and walked to try and find someone and no one seems to live round here at all. Then I saw your smoke and found... you.'

The creature smiled, but it was not a pleasant smile. He had horrible black teeth which made Nikki pull a face. 'You don't believe in fairies then?' he said.

'No. All that stuff is stupid. Only human beings and animal are real,' Nikki said.

'So what do you think I am?' he chuckled.

'I don't know. Some kind of circus freak?'

'Wrong.'

'Well, what are you then?' Nikki demanded, feeling slightly less sure of herself now.

'First tell me, what happened to your friends who were playing the fairy game?'

'They are *not* my friends for a start!' Nikki said, pulling another face. 'They seemed to just disappear. I guess that the same weird thing that happened to me, happened to them too.'

The creature nodded his head slowly. 'And where are they now?'

'Well, I don't know. If I knew that, I wouldn't be wandering round here on my own, would I?'

The creature shrugged. 'And what is your name and the names of your... the others?'

'Why should I tell you?' Nikki asked.

'Because, human child, I can help you get... home.'

Nikki hesitated, then said. 'I'm Nikki and *they* are Ellie and Lucy.'

The creature's eyes widened. 'And they are not your friends?'

'No! They are not!'

The creature nodded his head. 'Welcome to the Fairy World, Nikki. I am a goblin. My name is Grizzle.'

Chapter Three

Acantha

Lucan returned to the locked tower room; a scowl on his face. Every day he practised his archery and rode his horse. These things he loved, but he was not happy to be locked up once again with this dreary princess. It had been many days now and his father was still insisting that he spend time with her. He had long since stopped trying to talk to her, so he picked up a large book and hid his face behind it.

Gabriella had spent her days looking out of the window. She had tried to read some of the books that lined the bookshelves of this large stately room, but they seemed miserable to her. Many of them were about goblins and evil wizards. She didn't want to look at such things, so she gazed out of the window and longed for rescue. Her thoughts had often turned to Ellie and Lucy, Perizam and Silveria, and how they had rescued her parents from this castle some time ago. She daydreamed of what Ellie might be doing and wished she could contact her. Ellie was brave. Gabriella knew she would come. But there was no means to get a message out of the castle. She longed to see her parents and every day she scanned the horizon for sight of some rescue party, or even a messenger from Elysia.

As the days had gone by, more than anything, she was bored. She had often watched Lucan sulking behind a book. She knew he wasn't really concentrating on it, as he rarely turned a page. Sometimes he returned from his visits outside looking as much afraid as she was. But most of the time he was angry. He sometimes threw books or objects at the wall, or stomped around the room, shouting. Gabriella began to feel almost more sorry for Maleaver's son than she did for herself.

Today she was so fed up that she decided to speak to him. 'What are you reading?'

Lucan was shocked to hear her voice. He looked over the top of his book, then back to it without replying.

She tried again. 'I wish I could go outside like you do. What do you do when you're away from this room?'

Lucan smirked. 'I ride my horse and practise my archery.'

Gabriella sighed. 'You're so lucky.'

'Huh! You think so!' he mumbled.

'Yes! At least you get out of here. I love riding and archery. But I'm a prisoner here. You're not... at least, I don't think you are.' There was a pause. Lucan slid behind his book again. 'Are you?' Gabriella asked.

'Of course I'm not! Why should I be a prisoner? I'm Lord Maleaver's son,' Lucan declared, slamming the book on the table in front of him.

'Of course,' Gabriella said. She turned to look out of the window again. Lucan got up and approached her.

'Look, if you start being nice to me and doing what my father commands, you could have some time out of here too.'

'I'd like that,' Gabriella said. 'But why does he lock you in here?'

Lucan scowled again. 'I'm not really locked in here. The locks are to keep you from trying to escape. I can come and go as I please.'

Gabriella knew this wasn't true. She looked him in the eye for the first time. Lucan did not turn away. 'He's not very nice to you, is he?' she said.

Lucan shrugged and looked at his feet. 'He's my father. I must do as he tells me.'

'Even if he's cruel to you?'

Lucan walked back across the room. 'He says I need discipline. He says my school didn't teach me respect.'

'Is that where you've been until now?' Gabriella asked.

Lucan turned back to face her. 'Yes. It wasn't a bad place. I learnt so much and we got to do all sorts of sports and music.' His face lit up, then crumpled. 'I wish I was still there.'

'I love music too,' Gabriella said, smiling for the first time. 'Do you play an instrument?'

'I did play the lute when I was at school. But Father doesn't like music. And I love to sing. My mother used to sing to me.' A shadow came over his face.

Gabriella frowned. 'Where is she? Don't you see her anymore?'

'She died when I was three or four. One day she was there – sweet, smiling, playing with me – and the next she was gone. Dead. Father said it was a terrible tragedy but he didn't tell me what had happened to her. There was a big funeral and then I was sent off to school. I haven't been back here for many years.'

Gabriella felt strangely moved, watching Lucan's face, as he spoke of his mother. 'What did she sing to you?' she asked, gently.

'Lots of things, but the one I recall the best is a song about a river. She sang it to me so often I guess. I would drift off to sleep as she sang.'

'Can you sing it to me?' Gabriella asked.

Lucan looked around as if fearful of being overheard.

'It's ok. No one will hear you if you sing it softly,' Gabriella reassured him. She stood up and came towards him, sitting on a sofa in front of him, ready to listen.

Lucan made an uncomfortable face, but then he closed his eyes and hesitantly began to sing. *'Heavenly water gently flowing*

Never ceasing, watching me.
Murmured whispers hurry onward
Telling secrets to the sea.'

'It's beautiful,' whispered Gabriella. 'Is there more?'

'I think there was, but that's the only bit I remember,' he said. 'Look, I know you don't like me. There's not really much to like. But if you play along with my father's wishes and speak to me and pretend to be doing what I tell you, I'm sure he'd let you out of this room for a while. I could probably persuade him,' Lucan said.

Gabriella shrugged. 'I don't know.' This time she got up and walked away. 'He wants us to marry, so that he can rule my kingdom through you. I can't let that happen. What will he do to my parents?'

At that moment there was a grinding of the lock and Maleaver strode into the room. Immediately he noticed that there was a different atmosphere and looked from one to the other with a self satisfied smile on his face. 'Have you two been communicating?'

A fleeting look passed between Gabriella and Lucan.

'Ha! So, my son is winning you over. Well, well, the boy has some charm after all,' he said, taking Lucan's face in his hands and squeezing it.' Then he strode over to Gabriella. 'When I see evidence of you changing your attitude to my son I will be very pleased with you, little princess. The wife of a great Lord needs to learn how to behave towards him.' He pulled Gabriella up by her arm. His grip was so tight that she winced with pain, but didn't cry out. Maleaver pulled her across the room to where Lucan sat. 'Now, kneel to your lord,' he said to Gabriella. She dared a glance at Lucan.

Lucan looked uncomfortable. 'My Lord Father, it is really not...'

'Silence boy!' Maleaver cried.

Gabriella decided to play along – for both their sakes. She knelt before Lucan.

'That's better,' Maleaver said. 'Now, your reward boy is a little more time to yourself.' With that he whisked Lucan from the room. Gabriella picked up the book Lucan had been reading and hurled it at the door.

Early in the morning Perizam woke Lucy and Ellie. 'Come, dear ones, it is time to be on your way.' He had laid out some more appropriate clothes for them, so that they would blend in with the folks in the Borderlands between Elysia and Morteribus. They felt almost fairy-like when they put them on.

The smell of fish, smoking over the fire, filled the house. It was strange how quickly they had become accustomed to it again. It was homely and made them feel safe. They drank steaming cups of holmi as they sat in silence, listening to their own thoughts. Eventually Perizam handed them two small backpacks containing provisions.

'I also have this for you,' he said, handing Ellie a small vial of golden dust. 'Queen Hermia sent it in the hope that you would come. It will afford you a little magic if you need it. Sprinkle it where it is needed and wish for what you need. She hopes it will work, even though you are human. If the dust she sent to get you here worked, then I'm sure this will too.'

They hugged Perizam. Lucy felt hot tears spring into her eyes but she fought them back. 'I wish you were coming, Perizam,' she said.

'You will be fine without me, Lucy. You are brave and have many skills. All I have to offer is a little foresight sometimes, otherwise I am just a burden. You are a great thinker. Ellie needs you.'

He turned to Ellie. 'And you Ellie. You are brave too. Remember that you have your own kind of magic in this world, which has worked against the mighty Maleaver before. You can do it again. Princess Gabriella is depending on you.'

Ellie nodded. It was good to be reminded of this. 'I wish you were coming too,' she said quietly.

'There's a map in your backpack. Keep it to hand and follow the route I showed you. Although your mission is urgent, you must remember to rest along the way. It is a long quest to which you have been summoned. My thoughts go with you. If you need them just think hard about me and something will come to your mind.' He pressed some coins into Ellie's hand. 'A few shemels if you need them.'

With a last hug the girls set off in the direction Perizam had shown them. He stood at the door until they had gone over the brow of the hill and out of sight. 'Be safe little ones,' he whispered.

At first they walked in silence; the hills and woods stretching on into the distance in a never ending landscape. The boots they wore felt incredibly comfortable, as if they had been made just for them. After a while they stopped for a drink, as the sun rose higher in the sky and began to get hot.

'Last time we were here it was so dull all the time,' said Lucy. 'Do you remember the curse Maleaver had put on the land?'

'Mmm,' Ellie murmured, as she took a gulp of the water. 'I think it will get darker as we get nearer to Morteribus. If Maleaver's plan to rule Elysia succeeds, I expect he will make the whole country gloomy again.'

'That would be awful,' Lucy said. 'We must free Gabriella. But I feel so... '

'Scared?' suggested Ellie.

'Yes, but also... small. I mean, what can we do on our own? Last time we had Perizam, Silveria and Gabriella to help us. This time it's just me and you: Two kids from England. How could Queen Hermia possibly have thought we could save Gabriella?'

'I don't know Lucy, but she does. She believes in us. And we have to believe in ourselves or we've already let Maleaver win. Something will happen; some help will come, you'll see.' Ellie did her best to reassure Lucy, but she was fighting doubts herself.

The shadows lengthened and the day marched towards sunset. Ellie kept the map in front of her, but things looked different in real life than they did on a piece of paper. Just then, Ellie saw something moving near a stile, over the stone wall in the distance. At first she thought it might be an animal, but as they drew closer she realised it was not. Lucy had seen it too. Approaching cautiously, they found a fairy sitting on the wall, wailing. The fairy was shorter than both of them and wore little round spectacles. She didn't even look up as Ellie and Lucy stopped beside her, but kept on crying and blowing her nose into a very wet handkerchief.

'Hello,' said Ellie. 'What's wrong? Can we help you?'

Aware of their presence for the first time, the fairy frowned, shook her head and went back to her crying.

Ellie raised her eyebrows at Lucy.

'Are you lost?' Lucy asked. 'We'd like to help you if we can. Would you like a drink of water?'

The fairy looked up and blinked hard several times. 'Yes please,' she said. Lucy passed her the flask. After the fairy had drunk deeply she sighed. 'You can't help me. I don't even know what I'm doing here anymore. And you aren't even fairies.'

'Who are you?' asked Ellie.

'My name is Acantha,' sniffed the fairy. Ellie and Lucy looked at each other, their eyes widening.

'That's a good start,' said Lucy, smiling to reassure the fairy. 'But you say you don't know what you're doing here. Do you know Queen Hermia?'

'Of course,' said Acantha. 'I work for her. And I'm sure I was doing something important for her, but now I can't remember, and I don't even know how to get back to Elysia.' She wiped her nose. 'How do you know the Queen? And... are you...humans?'

Ellie smiled. 'We are. We helped to rescue the Queen and Prince Lysander when Maleaver kidnapped them before. We're on a mission from the Queen too. In fact, we're on the same mission as you. We're on our way to find Princess Gabriella. Maleaver has kidnapped her and is going to marry her to his son so he can rule over Elysia.'

Acantha's eyes widened in horror. 'How terrible! But I still can't remember any of it.'

'Use the dust, Ellie,' Lucy said. 'We need Acantha to remember. She might know something important.'

Ellie pulled the little tube of dust from her backpack. 'We'll try to bring back your memory,' she said. She sprinkled some dust over Acantha and wished hard for her memory to return. Lucy also wished hard, hoping to add force to the magic somehow. They waited and watched the fairy.

Acantha began. 'I was with two others – Fychan and Adalira.' She paused, her eyes flicked around as if searching inside her mind. 'We were ambushed by goblins. They took us by surprise, making sure we didn't have a chance to do any magic. Then they put goblin spells on us and ran off with the other two.'

'Was Grizzle with them?' Lucy asked. 'He was their leader.'

'I don't know, but they knew what they were doing,' Acantha said.

Ellie looked at the sun. 'It's getting late. Why don't you come with us. We're going to make camp. We could do with your help Acantha.'

Acantha got down from the wall and they set off towards a wood. 'This is where I think Perizam said we should make our first camp. We can make a fire without it being too obvious and set up a shelter.'

Lucy felt a shiver go through her as they entered the wood. The sun would soon set and it would be very dark. At Brownie camp she had watched Brown Owl make a fire by rubbing sticks in a certain way. Brown Owl had said it was very difficult and not many people could do it. It had taken ages but eventually smoke had started to rise and a fire had gradually come alive. Lucy had been fascinated and when she had returned home she had tried it several times in her garden, with her dad's help. At first she had not been able to do it, but she wasn't one to give up and finally, after several attempts, she had done it. But only once. Now she was going to try it again. She, Ellie and Acantha hunted for dry leaves and things that would catch alight easily. They also found a stick to be a drill and a piece of wood to twist the drill into. Then Lucy made a bendy stick into a bow using her shoelace. She twisted the drill into the string of the bow and used the bow to spin the drill in the block of wood. This was the tiring part. She and Ellie took turns to keep it going while Acantha gathered more wood. After a while, smoke began to rise from the dry leaves that were next to the block of wood. As the smoke began to get thicker, Lucy gently blew into the leaves.

'Come on, come on,' Ellie whispered – willing it to take a light.

Suddenly, a flame leapt up from the dry leaves. Lucy fell back in shock.

'You did it!' Ellie exclaimed. 'Well done Lucy!' She gave Lucy an enormous hug.

'Now we need to build it up carefully with more sticks,' Lucy said, secretly feeling very pleased with herself.

Ellie and Acantha set up the shelter using the piece of waterproof skin that Perizam had given them and some large branches. The three of them huddled together near the fire and ate some of the food from their back packs.

Not far away, in the same woods, Nikki and Grizzle were sitting around Grizzle's fire. Grizzle had decided to let Nikki sleep in his shelter last night and he had made another smaller one for himself. Nikki was excited. He had been telling her of a wonderful castle that he was going to take her to. In the castle lived a great Lord called Maleaver. Grizzle had told her that he himself was Captain of the goblins – leading them like a great army in the service of this Lord. He was just having a holiday at the moment. Strange holiday, Nikki had thought. Grizzle told her that Maleaver would welcome them with a banquet and give Nikki a luxurious suite of rooms (with golden chairs, a four poster bed and diamond studded taps in the bathroom!) In return, all he would require was information about Ellie and Lucy. She was looking forward to a comfy bed and some decent food. And maybe, just maybe, this would be an excellent way to pay Ellie and Lucy back.

Grizzle had not told Nikki that Maleaver had banished him from his service when he had failed to stop Ellie, Lucy and Gabriella rescuing Queen Hermia and Prince Lysander. He was hatching a plan. Thinking that Maleaver would be so pleased that he had brought him valuable information and a useful prisoner, he hoped that he would get his job back. He was going to go to sleep happy for the first time in a long while.

Chapter 4

Adalira

As the sun rose, Ellie, Lucy and Acantha were already up. None of them had slept well. As the fire had died down they had become very cold, even though they huddled together. They were also anxious to get on their way towards Morteribus.

Ellie looked at the map. 'We need to keep heading west. We can pass through this little town here called Drewdale. We might even find a place to stay the night.'

The day was hot again and they used up a lot of their water. Acantha flew some of the time, which was helpful as she could go on ahead and tell the girls what was coming up.

It was late afternoon when Acantha came flying back to tell them that the town was just over the brow of the hill. Ellie was surprised but pleased that her map reading had been so accurate. She wondered if Perizam was somehow guiding her.

The place consisted of a few cottages leading along a track to a town square. The buildings here were larger, with two or three storeys. At ground level a colonnade of arches ran around the square, underneath the upper levels. It reminded Ellie of an old-fashioned town they had visited last year on holiday in France. The cobbled square was set up with market stalls selling fruit and vegetables, cloth, jewellery, household items and much more. There were a lot of people milling around. Some were ordinary Borderlands folk dressed in similar clothes to Ellie and Lucy. There were fairies and dryads, as well as a few other strange looking creatures that Lucy recognised from stories she had read: Nymphs, dwarves and even a satyr. Horses were tethered around the square and cafes were open under the colonnade. Lucy longed to sit in the shade and drink a large cool glass of lemonade.

'Let's sit down,' Acantha said, as if reading Lucy's mind. 'We deserve a rest.'

'We need to get some food for the journey and look for a place to stay,' Ellie said.

'I think we have time for a rest first. These stalls don't look like they're packing up for a while; it's too busy,' Acantha said.

Lucy's face lit up as Acantha led them to a pretty looking cafe and they sat down at a table in the shade. Almost at once a girl came to ask what they would like to drink. Amidst the strange sounding drinks on the menu, like Asthme, Ichorio and Walsasha, there was Homemade Lemonade. The girls ordered this, whilst Acantha ordered a glass of Eritho – or red berry juice, as Acantha informed them.

It was pleasant just to sit still and watch the hustle and bustle of the market square. A juggler had begun a routine and a crowd was gathering around him. The girls could see the balls and sticks and fire brands flying up into the air, over the heads of the crowd. Then music began and a band of travelling minstrels emerged into the square. Dressed in brightly coloured clothing, they played a bodhran, a lute, two fiddles, two whistles and a small harp called a lyre. They danced and sang as well and the crowd clapped and danced along too. The music was enchanting and Lucy almost got up to dance herself.

Suddenly Acantha stood up. 'That's Adalira!'

'Where?' Ellie asked.

'There. The one playing the lyre. I'm sure of it.'

'We should go and talk to her,' said Ellie. 'What is she doing with those musicians?'

'I don't know. Maybe she escaped from the goblins,' said Acantha.

'But surely she would have continued with her mission,' Lucy said.

'I'm going to find out,' Acantha said. 'Wait here.'

The minstrels were winding their way out of the square, having collected money from the appreciative crowd. Adalira was on the end as they danced their way down a side street.

'Adalira!' Acantha called. 'Adalira! Wait! It's me, Acantha. I need to talk to you.'

At first Adalira continued on, not seeming to notice. but Acantha managed to catch her up by flying.

'Adalira!'

Adalira stopped and looked at Acantha as if she had seen a ghost. The minstrels continued on.

'Go away!' hissed Adalira. 'I'm busy.'

'Adalira, what happened to you? Why are you with these minstrels?'

'Go away! I don't know you.' Adalira tried to follow the minstrels, but Acantha held her back.

'Adalira, don't you remember the mission to rescue Princess Gabriella? The goblins kidnapped you and Fychan. Have you lost your memory too?' said Acantha.

Adalira tried to shake her off. 'If you don't let me go I'll...'

'Put a spell on me with your magic lyre? No you won't. Remember, I am immune to it. I have sung my song to it. It knows me,' said Acantha sternly.

The street was empty now. 'Well I'm not coming with you. I like travelling with the minstrels.' She looked around as if to make sure no one would overhear her. 'I don't want to go to Morteribus. It's too dangerous. Leave me alone.'

'So, you do remember then?' Acantha said.

'Yes I remember, but the goblins frightened me and told me I'd be happier with the minstrels and you know what? I am, so go away!'

With that, Adalira pulled herself from Acantha's grip and flew off to join the minstrels.

Acantha returned to Ellie and Lucy.

'What shall we do?' asked Ellie.

'She's a stubborn young fairy!' said Acantha.

'We could do with her help,' Lucy said. 'Isn't her lyre magical?'

'Yes,' Acantha said. 'It has the power to put people into a deep sleep, or to make them dance; unable to do anything else for hours, depending on what tune she plays. You can only gain immunity if you sing it a song that it has not heard before; your own original song. You two will need to think of one and be ready to sing it if we are to get Adalira to come with us.'

'How are we going to do that?' asked Lucy.

'We'll have to get her away from the minstrels,' said Acantha. 'I saw the direction they took. They'll probably make camp somewhere for the night. Let's buy food and follow them.'

Lucy's hopes of a warm comfy bed for the night began to fade.

The minstrels made camp at the roadside, near a stream. They built a fire and sat around it for a while singing and telling stories. Acantha, Ellie and Lucy bought their food and set out to look for them. After a while, they saw the camp up ahead and hid themselves behind a stone wall, a short distance away.

'Okay, everyone know what to do?' said Acantha.

Lucy and Ellie nodded.

Lucy stepped out onto the road and walked towards the minstrel camp. She took deep breaths, as she rehearsed in her head what she was going to say. The minstrels looked towards her as she approached.

'Good evening,' she said, smiling. She noticed that there was only one fairy among them and saw the lyre at her feet.

'Good evening,' one of the minstrels replied. Others nodded to her and greeted her.

'I heard you all playing in the market square today. You make beautiful music.'

'Thank you,' said the man who had answered her. They didn't invite her to join them and there was an uneasy silence.

'I've always wanted to play the lyre,' Lucy said, looking over to Adalira. 'I wondered if you would be so kind as to let me have a go. Maybe teach me a little tune?'

Adalira looked at her suspiciously. The other minstrels were watching her closely. 'Well... I don't know...'

'I'd really love it if you would. I have some shemels to pay for your trouble.'

Adalira looked at the others. 'I don't think so. We're finished performing for the day.'

Lucy's heart beat faster as she put on her most disappointed face. 'I'm sorry if I'm interrupting. I'll just be on my way. Your music was lovely today. Thank you. Goodbye.' She began to walk away, hoping her bluff would work.

'Wait!' Adalira called. Lucy breathed a sigh of relief as she heard Adalira coming after her. 'I'm being rude. Sorry. Come back and I'll show you some tunes. You could stay with us for the night if you like.'

'Are you sure? Well, thank you. I'm grateful. But... I'm quite shy. Would you mind if we went a little way off from the others while I learn. I don't want to sound terrible in front of all those brilliant musicians.'

Adalira laughed. 'You don't need to worry. Nobody will mind.'

'Even so...' said Lucy, biting her lip.

'I guess it will be okay,' Adalira said, glancing back at the group, who were looking towards her. Now all Lucy had to do was guide her towards where Ellie and Acantha had arranged to hide, just around the bend in the road. 'I'm sure we're far enough away now,' said Adalira before they reached the bend.

'Just a little further,' Lucy said, looking back at the minstrels. 'Do you mind? I don't want to be watched.'

Adalira frowned, but followed Lucy, gripping her lyre. As soon as they rounded the bend Ellie jumped down from a tree, giving them both a shock. Acantha flew down behind Adalira.

'You tricked me!' Adalira shouted at Lucy.

'Adalira,' Acantha said, firmly, 'You have to come with us. Queen Hermia is relying on us to save the princess and all of Elysia. Don't you care about that?'

'Not anymore!' cried Adalira. 'And you can't force me!' She began to strum her fingers across the lyre.

'Lucy, Ellie – sing your songs to the lyre now. This is the sleeping tune.'

Immediately, Lucy began to sing. Her voice was sweet and tuneful and she had no trouble making up a song about home. Ellie faltered. She had never been any good at singing. She thought she sounded like a croaky old lady when she sang. She began to feel drowsy and started to sway.

'Sing Ellie!' said Acantha, trying to grab the lyre from Adalira.

Adalira danced away from her, laughing. Acantha tried again. 'Adalira, you know we're not meant to use our magic on each other but you are forcing me to do this.' She lifted her arms and flung fairy dust over her friend. At once Adalira froze, but it was too late for Ellie, she slumped to the ground.

'Ellie!' Lucy gasped, bending down to her friend.

Suddenly they heard a noise, like a strange hissing, coming towards them. Acantha flew to look and saw the minstrels coming up the road. They looked different somehow and Acantha realised, in horror, that their faces were no longer those of woodland folk. They had distorted into the dark faces of changeling shadow people. Myths and legends from the Borderlands, told of clans of dark shadow people, who could change into any form they liked. And in that form they often trapped unsuspecting fairy folk in order to make them into shadow people too. Acantha realised all at once that Adalira had been under their spell.

'Quickly!' she said to Lucy, we have to get out of here. 'Those minstrels are not minstrels at all. They're shadow people.'

She flung more dust over Adalira, who blinked rapidly and put her fingers back to her lyre. 'There's no time for that!' shouted Acantha. 'Those minstrels are shadow people. We have to get out of here.'

Adalira gasped.

'Wake Ellie up, Adalira!' Lucy cried.

'I can't. The magic is too powerful. She will be asleep for a few hours now.'

'Can't you do anything?' pleaded Lucy. The hissing was getting closer.

'We can use magic to make her lighter and carry her with us. I think we'll have to use it on you too Lucy and carry you. I don't think you can outrun them now.'

Adalira and Acantha sprinkled Lucy and Ellie with fairy dust just as the shadow people rounded the corner. The hissing became angrier. For a moment Lucy looked into their shadowy faces and felt a scream rise to her lips. As they reached out their shadowy arms towards the girls the magic began to work. Lucy and Ellie lifted off the ground and the two fairies grabbed hold of them and began to fly as fast as they could. The shadow people began to move faster, hovering just above the ground.

'Hurry!' Lucy cried, as the shadow people appeared to be gaining on them.

The fairies flew as fast as they could and began to widen the gap between them and the shadow people. The sun had almost set when they found some caves set into a clump of rocks.

'In here,' said Acantha.

It was pitch black in the cave. 'Do we have to?' Lucy asked, as Acantha placed her feet on the ground.

'The shadow people won't come in here. They can't go into total darkness because they get lost and fade into nothing.'

Lucy didn't want to step into total darkness either, but she accepted that they had to do it. The cave went back a long way. The two fairies flew cautiously into the darkness and placed Ellie's sleeping body gently on the ground. They had luminous veins in their wings that gave off a pale blue glow. Lucy followed with her arms out in front of her, so that she didn't bump into anything. She could feel the jagged edges of the cave just above her head. As they sat down, the fairies folded their wings behind them and all the light disappeared. It was pitch black. They all held hands and Lucy closed her eyes, pretending and wishing she was at home in bed.

It seemed like they had been sitting in the darkness for hours when Ellie began to stir and groan. 'Where am I? I can't see!'

'Ellie,' Lucy whispered. 'It's okay. Just keep quiet. We're in a cave. I'll explain later. We have to be very quiet though.' Lucy reached out for Ellie's hand and when she found it she squeezed it.

Suddenly, there was a rustling at the front of the cave. Everyone tensed. The shadow people!

'Go away, go away, go away!' Lucy chanted in her head. But the noise came further into the cave. Then they heard a voice.

'This will do. We'll camp here for the night. I'll start a fire.'

Lucy recognised the voice at once – it was Grizzle!

Chapter 5

Escape

Lucy stifled a gasp, as Ellie leaned over and whispered, 'It's Grizzle!'

'I know,' said Lucy, feeling the goose bumps rising on her skin.

'You mean Maleaver's captain of goblins?' asked Acantha. 'The one who kidnapped Princess Gabriella last time?'

'Yes,' Lucy said.

They listened and waited as there were more scuffling noises at the front of the cave. Grizzle was making the fire.

'I hope he doesn't attract those shadow people,' said Lucy.

'I think they must have passed us by now,' Adalira said.

'Bring the wood over here,' they heard Grizzle say.

'How long does it take to make a fire?' came a grumpy female voice.

'It takes skill and time. Be patient,' Grizzle ordered.

'Well I'm cold,' the girl said. 'How long is it going to take to get to that castle? I hope we won't have to spend too many nights out in the cold.'

'Be quiet!' Grizzle commanded. 'Just bank up the firewood and get inside the cave. I'll have it lit soon enough.'

Ellie was puzzled. She leaned over to Lucy and whispered. 'That voice sounds familiar.'

'I know. If I didn't know it was impossible, I'd say it was Nikki Walters.'

'But how did *she* get here and what would she be doing with Grizzle?' wondered Ellie.

'Who is she?' Adalira asked.

'Nikki Walters is a girl from our school – not a very nice girl,' said Lucy.

'Shh! Someone is coming towards the back of the cave!' Acantha said.

A shuffling noise alerted them, as someone groped around in the dark.

'Where are you going?' said Grizzle. 'Watch out for the creatures that often lurk in these caves!' He chuckled to himself. Nikki stopped and moved back towards the entrance.

Lucy shivered at the thought of what else might be with them, here in the dark. Everyone was feeling cold now.

'We can't stay here for the night, it's too cold,' whispered Acantha. 'We can't make a fire now that they're here, and they might see us once their fire is lit.'

'I have to know who that other person is,' Ellie said. 'It sounds so like Nikki. I'm going to look.'

'Ellie, no! Stay here. If Grizzle finds us...'

'I'll be careful – they won't know I'm here.'

Ellie crept on her hands and knees towards the sounds of Grizzle straining to make the fire. As she moved closer to the entrance, some light filtered into the cave, but as it was nearly dark outside it didn't help much. She felt her way along the wall. It was muddy, and damp leaves stuck to her hands and knees. She thought fleetingly of her little brother – how much he would enjoy getting this dirty – and a lump came into her throat. She swallowed hard and tried to concentrate.

Suddenly, there was a little flare as the moss and twigs burst into flame. Ellie could smell the smoke. She stopped as Grizzle fed the fire more bits of bush and wood to make the flame grow. She could see his shadowy figure now, bent over the dancing flames. Near him, huddled in a cloak, sat a girl. Ellie couldn't quite see her face. She crept closer but didn't see a ledge jutting out of the wall in front of her.

'Ouch!' she exclaimed. Grizzle and his companion looked up. Ellie slunk back and pressed herself into the shadows.

'What was that?' said the person in the cloak.

'I don't know,' Grizzle said, peering back into the darkness of the cave. 'If there are animals back there, the fire should keep them away from us.'

The other person stood up and came as close as she could to the fire. 'Well I don't like it here, Grizzle.'

'Stop your whining, human,' Grizzle said. 'It's too dark to move now and I've spent ages getting this fire to light. Sit there and be quiet.'

Ellie strained to see who was with Grizzle. The light from the fire illuminated the person's face for a few seconds as she turned to sit down.

Ellie's eyes widened and she pulled back as far as she could. It *was* Nikki. How could Nikki Walters possibly be here?

'We'll start out at dawn for the castle. It's still a long way. Then you can tell Lord Maleaver all you know about your little friends being here.' Grizzle knew the quickest route, but he didn't want Nikki to think it would be a short journey. And he couldn't bear more of her whining.

'I told you before – they're not my friends!' Nikki said.

'I know! Lord Maleaver will be pleased with us. He will be able to alert the castle guard to watch out for them. They're bound to be on their way to free the princess. They think they're invincible! Stupid creatures!'

'They were talking about a princess when I was spying on them,' Nikki said.

'I heard that Maleaver has captured her and is going to marry her to that boy Lucan,' Grizzle said.

As silently as she could, Ellie crept back to the others and whispered to them what she had overheard. 'We have to get out of here and get to the castle,' Ellie said. 'We don't want Maleaver to know we're coming.'

'How could Nikki be so stupid as to get involved with Grizzle?' Lucy said.

'She doesn't know she's in danger! Maleaver hates humans after what we did last time,' Ellie said.

'We should wait until they are asleep and creep out past them,' said Adalira. 'I would use my lyre, but we can't until Ellie sings her song to it.'

Ellie grimaced at the thought. She was prepared to face Maleaver again, but the thought of singing in front of everyone made her feel sick.

It felt like they had to wait forever until they could hear Grizzle snoring loudly. Cautiously, they crept towards the front of the cave, hoping that Nikki was also asleep.

They were both sprawled across the entrance to the cave. Adalira and Acantha flew over the top of them whilst Ellie and Lucy climbed carefully past them, peering in disbelief at Nikki. Ellie felt a stab of anger that Nikki would be mean enough to betray them to Maleaver, but then Nikki didn't have a clue what she was getting herself into. For a moment, Ellie wondered if they should take Nikki with them, but she shook the thought from her mind, deciding that Gabriella needed her to stay focused. It was still a long way to Morteribus according to the map. The fairies led the way by the light of the luminous veins in their wings. It was cold and the girls pulled their cloaks tightly around them, trying to focus on the quest.

Gabriella's days began alone, then she was joined by Lucan in the afternoons. When Maleaver left them alone, they often laughed and enjoyed each other's company. They played Echamp (a game similar to Chess) and Dragons and Magicians (similar to Snakes and Ladders). When Maleaver was around, Gabriella did whatever he told her to do for Lucan, as if she was his servant, and Lucan pretended to be stern towards Gabriella. He hated treating her like this, but Gabriella had said he must do it if they wanted to gain more freedom and make Maleaver believe that his plan was working.

This morning, Gabriella was summoned to have breakfast with Lucan and Maleaver in the grand dining room. She glanced across at Lucan, keeping her face serious. He avoided looking at her.

'Good morning Princess. I trust you slept well,' Maleaver said.

'I did,' she replied.

'You will eat with us this morning, then you will spend the morning with Lucan.' He turned to his son. 'You will tell her what we expect of a royal wife and continue to train her to do your bidding.'

'Of course, my Lord Father,' Lucan said.

The rest of the breakfast was eaten in silence.

'Take the Princess into the garden, Lucan. The air will do her good. You are looking pale, Princess, and we can't have you fading away when the wedding is so close.'

Two guards accompanied them, but when they reached the walled garden Lucan insisted that they didn't need an escort, as there was no other way out of the garden than this one gate. The guards agreed to wait outside the gate for them. When they were alone, Lucan apologised, as he always did, for his behaviour in his father's presence.

'There's no need to be sorry, Lucan,' Gabriella said. 'I've told you, it's like we're in a play when your father's around. We're just acting the parts.'

'I know,' said Lucan, 'but it makes me mad to have to treat you like that. I wish my father had left me alone at school. I was happy there. And you would have been happy in Elysia.'

'Well, it's not your fault. You are a prisoner here as much as I am. Your father wants you to be like him, and you've tried to please him, but that's not who you are, Lucan. There is goodness in you that is not from him and it will overcome the darkness.'

Lucan sighed. 'I hope so.'

'I wish help would come,' Gabriella said. 'I don't understand it. My mother and father should have sent out a rescue party. Oh, I wish Ellie and Lucy were here.'

'Tell me more about them,' Lucan said. 'It must be very strange to have friends from the human world. And I really don't understand how they could resist my father's magic.'

'Neither do I, but Ellie seems to have special powers of her own,' Gabriella said.

Lucan frowned. 'I thought humans were dull creatures with no magic.'

'I'm not sure it is magic,' Gabriella said. 'Ellie was just... brave.'

They walked on in silence for a while. Gabriella picked a drooping flower and began to twirl it in her fingers.

'Lucan, what would you say to us trying to escape ourselves?'

'I'd say – how?'

'I don't know yet, but we could try.' She hesitated. 'I like you a lot Lucan, but I don't want to get married.'

'No, neither do I.'

'And you hate being here as much as I do. So it's worth a try, isn't it?'

'I guess so. But everywhere is so heavily guarded. They only let us in here alone because there's a wall all the way round and there are guards on the only gate.'

'I wish I could do magic here, but your father has put one of his powerful spells on me. Do you know any magic Lucan?'

He looked away. 'I did. At school, magic was one of our daily lessons. But... it was mainly dark magic.

My father insisted that I learn it. Then one day... well, something happened.'

He went quiet and Gabriella waited. 'You don't have to tell me if you don't want to,' she said.

'No, I do. I used the dark magic on a friend who had fallen out with me. He was my best friend, but we had had an argument – a big one. So I got angry and threw some really bad magic at him. The effect was only supposed to last a short while, but he disappeared and never returned. No one knew what had happened to him and I never admitted it was me. I was afraid of my father if I got thrown out of school. So instead I stopped listening in magic class and I promised myself I would never use magic again.'

'You poor thing!' Gabriella said. 'Magic can be used for such good in the right hands.'

'I know. But I don't trust myself. There is too much of my father in me.'

'I wish we knew who your mother was. Don't you even know her name?'

'No. My father refuses to tell me. And she was just Mummy to me.'

Lucan looked so sad that Gabriella wanted to hug him, but thought he might not appreciate it. Instead she pushed him playfully. 'Come on I'll race you round the garden and back to that apple tree. Wish I could fly here –I'd win easily!' She set off, laughing.

'Hey, what about ready, steady, go!' Lucan said, laughing too and running after her.

Lucan soon overtook Gabriella, but as they rounded a corner Gabriella came to a sudden stop. 'Hey Lucan,' she called 'Come and look at this.'

Lucan back tracked and found her peering up at a strong vine growing up the wall.

'Is this an outside wall?' Gabriella asked.

'I think it backs onto the parkland where Father grazes his horses,' Lucan said.

'Do you think we could climb it?'

'Possibly, but what about the drop on the other side?' Lucan said. The wall was three times as tall as they were.

'Could you get some rope? If we brought some rope we could tie it to the top of the vine, dangle it down the outside of the wall and climb down. Then we could run through the horses' field and over the fence into the woods. We've been in here an hour already, so they're not likely to come looking for us straight away. We could get a good head start.'

Lucan looked uncertain.

Gabriella found herself growing impatient. 'Please Lucan, we can't just sit here and let it all go ahead. If no one is coming to rescue me I'll have to rescue myself, and I'm doing it with or without you.'

Lucan admired her determination. 'I'll bring the rope. I'll help you.'

'Will you come with me?'

His chewed his lip.

'They'll know you helped me,' she said.

He nodded. 'I'll come.'

Chapter 6

Fychan

Ellie, Lucy and the fairies travelled for what seemed endless days and nights. This morning they fell into a pile of soft mossy grass. Even though it was wet with dew, they didn't care. They were soon fast asleep.

When they awoke, the sun was high in the sky. It warmed their skin and dried out their clothes.

Anxiously, Ellie pulled out the map. 'I'm not sure we've stayed on course.'

Lucy studied the map for a while and looked around to see if she could work out where they were. 'Perhaps if we try to find the river we could follow it.'

'But how will we know it's the right river?' asked Adalira.

Ellie closed her eyes and wished Perizam was with them. Gradually a picture came to her mind, of herself sitting in Perizam's house with him. They were drinking holmi by the fire. Ellie felt warm and happy. 'Lucy's idea is a good one,' Perizam was saying. 'Head west now towards that rocky outcrop you can see on the hill in the distance. You're doing well child.' He smiled at her and then the picture began to fade.

Ellie opened her eyes. 'Lucy's right, we should follow the river.'

Everyone was surprised by Ellie's certainty as she led them towards the rocky outcrop. Adalira grumbled a little, but Acantha told her to be quiet and trust Ellie.

'How come you're so sure this is the right way?' Lucy whispered to Ellie as they walked.

Ellie smiled. 'Perizam is guiding us.'

At once Lucy was happy, knowing that her dear friend Perizam was still able to help them.

It was hard to keep walking when they were so tired, but by mid afternoon they had climbed the hill and were looking down over a magnificent waterfall. The water roared as it cascaded over the top of the rocks.

'Let's get down to the bottom. Perhaps we can swim. I could do with it. I feel really dirty,' Ellie said.

Climbing carefully down the side of the waterfall, they could hear a faint noise, like singing. As they looked into the clear pool, at the bottom of the waterfall, they saw a small creature jumping, diving and playing. His melodious voice echoed around the walls of the valley, sometimes being drowned out by the noise of the tumbling waterfall.

'I know that voice!' exclaimed Adalira.

'Me too,' Acantha said.

'Who is he?' asked Lucy.

'It's Fychan,' laughed Adalira. 'He was with us on the rescue mission. He's a water nymph and I guess the goblins dumped him here to distract him.'

Fychan was totally unaware of his visitors as they drew nearer to him. Lucy was fascinated by the handsome, elf- like creature who kept disappearing under the water and resurfacing on the other side of the pool.

'Fychan!' Adalira called, but he didn't hear her. 'Fychan!'

'Fychan!' they all shouted together.

His singing stopped abruptly and he stared at them, wide-eyed, for a moment. Then he was gone; diving under the water as smoothly as a salmon.

'Where's he gone?' asked Ellie after several minutes. 'Can he breathe under water?'

'No, but he can hold his breath for a while,' Acantha replied. She looked around. 'There he is!' He was trying to hide behind the waterfall. 'I'm sure he recognised us.'

'We could get to him on that ledge,' Ellie said.

The fairies were not keen, as they couldn't get their wings wet. 'You wait here, we'll go,' Ellie said.

She and Lucy made their way carefully over the slippery rocks. 'Fychan, we're your friends,' she called out. But as he saw them approaching he leapt into the water. 'Oh well, I wanted a swim,' Ellie said. She took off her shoes and outer clothes and dived in after him. Lucy gasped. She didn't like the thought of plunging into that cold water.

Ellie swam around the pool, catching glimpses of Fychan from time to time, but he was too fast and could dive very deep. Eventually she had to give up and get out. At that moment Fychan surfaced on the other side, grinning at them.

Acantha stood with her hands on her hips and shouted at him. 'Now just you listen up Fychan. I've had enough of your fun and games! We were sent to find the princess Gabriella. Queen Hermia trusted you and we could do with your help. You get out of that pool this minute and come with us!'

'I'm not coming!' he shouted back. 'Leave me alone. I like it here and this is where I'm staying. So keep that creature out of my pool,' he said, pointing at Ellie.

'How dare you speak to Ellie like that! She and Lucy are very important people from the human world; summoned here by the Queen,' Acantha shouted.

'Well I don't care!' he shouted back and disappeared under the water again.

'This clearly isn't working,' Adalira said. 'We need to lure him out of the pool. The water is playing tricks on his mind.'

'But how can we do it?' asked Lucy.

Adalira looked around. A little distance away lay some of Fychan's things, including a bow and a quiver of arrows. 'Look! Fychan's bow. He's a fantastic archer. What if one of us were to shoot his bow and arrows. Maybe he'd try to stop us.'

'I've done some archery,' Lucy cried. 'Can I do it?'

Everyone looked at her in surprise. 'Okay,' said Acantha. 'If Fychan comes out, the rest of us will grab him to stop him getting back in the pool. Let's pretend for now that we are leaving, and Lucy spots the bow and stops to have a go. We can hide and ambush him.'

Fychan was furious when he saw Lucy using his bow. He stood in the water and shouted at her. 'What do you think you're doing? Put that down, it's mine! And it's dangerous in untrained hands.'

Lucy was enjoying herself, shooting arrows into a tree some distance away and not missing once. She couldn't help giggling to herself.

'Don't make me come out there!' he shouted.

'That's exactly what I want you to do,' Lucy said to herself.

Fychan heaved himself out of the water. All of a sudden his legs felt like heavy weights – he had been in the water for so long. 'Put my bow down, human!' he said, stomping towards Lucy. Lucy made to run away with the bow. Fychan started to run after her, but just as he was almost upon her, Ellie and the fairies pounced on him and he tumbled to the ground.

'What? Get off me!' he cried, squirming and twisting.

'No. Not until you see that we need you, Fychan!' Acantha said, as the others managed to keep him from escaping. He stopped struggling and lay on the ground looking up into Acantha's large wise eyes. It was as if a magic was leaving him and his heavy legs and arms felt lighter again. The girls noticed that his toes and fingers were webbed. Everyone peered anxiously at him as a big tear rolled down his cheek.

'I'm sorry, Acantha, Adalira. I don't know what I was thinking. My mind was fuddled by the beautiful waterfall pool. I'm sorry to you too... Ellie and...Lucy is it?'

The girls nodded. 'Don't cry,' Lucy said. 'We're just glad you're with us now. And I'm sorry I used your bow and arrows.'

Slowly they released him. As he stood up he shook Lucy's hand. 'You're actually a very good shot,' he said, grinning at Lucy. Lucy looked down at her feet and beamed. 'I'd be proud to have you on my archers' team.' He turned to Ellie. 'And you're not a bad swimmer.'

'Thanks,' she replied. 'Shall we have something to eat and keep going? I'm worried about Gabriella. I hope we get there in time to save her from the wedding and before Grizzle and Nikki get there to warn Maleaver that we're coming.'

Nikki and Grizzle arrived at the gates of Maleaver's castle. Nikki was impressed by the size of the great towering structure. There were four rectangular towers, one in each corner of the walls, but no moat. Turrets and towers of differing sizes poked out from above the high stone walls. There was a grey gloomy feel about the place that Nikki didn't really like.

They crossed through surrounding parkland belonging to Maleaver. As they approached the huge gates, Nikki shuddered. She was cold, but it was more than that. From behind the portcullis, the Gatekeeper barked the usual question: 'Who goes there?'

Grizzle mustered all his confidence and looked him in the eye. 'It is I – Grizzle. I have some very important and urgent news for Lord Maleaver.'

The Gatekeeper looked him up and down in disgust. 'You were banished months ago Grizzle. You look like a tramp and you smell even worse. Get along with you before I call the guards.'

Nikki looked at Grizzle in disbelief. This was not what he had told her. She had been looking forward to a luxurious room and a hot bath.

'I have some extremely important news that Lord Maleaver will want to hear,' Grizzle persisted. 'He will be furious if he finds out that you have stopped me from giving it.'

'Rubbish. He would be more furious if I let you in. Be off with you! Go crawl back to your little hovel in the woods.' The Gatekeeper turned to leave.

'Wait!' Nikki cried. The Gatekeeper turned and looked at her, as if she hadn't existed until now. 'Let *me* in to see Lord Maleaver then. When he finds out who I am and where I'm from he will be very interested.'

'And who are you? Where are you from?'

'My name is Nikki and I'm from the human world. I have news for him of a rescue attempt to snatch the princess.'

The Gatekeeper considered this for a while. 'Very well. You may come in.'

'And Grizzle?'

The Gatekeeper wrinkled his nose and thought for a moment. 'Very well then, although you both must be cleaned up before entering into the presence of Lord Maleaver.'

It was all Nikki could do to stop herself from hugging the Gatekeeper as the portcullis lifted and they were allowed to pass.

In the servants' quarters they were escorted to separate rooms and given cold water to wash in and fresh, servants' clothes. It was not quite what Nikki had been hoping for, but she decided that once they had given Maleaver their news she would receive the luxury she had been promised by Grizzle. She was annoyed with him for lying to her. A steward came to escort them to a long grand corridor, where they were told to wait. Nikki looked around in awe at the paintings and statues that lined the corridor. Grizzle muttered to himself as if preparing what he was going to say. For the first time since she had met him, he seemed nervous.

A tall golden door at the end of the corridor opened slowly. 'You may enter into Lord Maleaver's presence now,' said the steward.

Nikki's stomach began to churn as Grizzle led the way. He walked with his head down and when he reached the throne on which Maleaver sat, he made a low bow. Nikki did the same. They stayed bowed before Maleaver until he said, 'You may look at me.' Nikki was surprised to look into a harsh but handsome face. Maleaver looked them both up and down.

'So, Grizzle. You dare to return to my castle. You must have brought me something I want very badly.'

'Yes my Lord. I have brought you important news. And I have brought you this,' he pulled Nikki forward.

Maleaver raised his eyebrows. 'A human. And what would I want with it?'

'My Lord, it has news that the other humans, who came before, are back, and most likely on their way to rescue the princess,' Grizzle said.

Maleaver let out a roaring laugh that made them both jump. 'Is this your urgent news? Well, I have no fear of them! My castle is well defended. They don't stand a chance of getting in this time. As for this human... What do you know of the two who came before?'

Nikki swallowed hard and tried to speak normally, but her throat felt like it was full of sand. She cleared it. 'I know they came here on purpose and I followed them. I wanted to know what they were up to. They had some kind of letter and were talking about fairy princesses, which I thought was strange because Ellie is so not into that sort of thing and....'

'Silence!' Maleaver commanded. 'And why would you – a fellow human, want to betray them to me?'

'They're sneaky and I want to get my own back on them for a few things.'

Maleaver laughed again. 'And you'd like me to help you would you?'

'No, I'd like to help you,' Nikki said, trying to be bold. 'In return for a nice room in your palace.'

Maleaver stopped laughing. 'You want to bargain with me?'

Grizzle could see that this was not going his way. 'My Lord, let me have my position as Goblin leader back. I can lead a party out to capture the humans. They can't be far from the castle now. Then you can be rid of them forever.'

Maleaver stood up. His face was a black storm cloud, as he roared, 'I do not make bargains with filthy little worms such as you!'

85

Nikki and Grizzle cowered, fearing that Maleaver may be about to do something horrible to them. But he sat down again. 'However, I will give you this chance to prove yourselves worthy of not being turned to stone! I am sending you out to find them and bring them to me. The wedding, between my son and the princess, is set for the day after tomorrow. You have until then. Otherwise the goblins will have instructions to bring you both back here as my prisoners. Got it?'

Nikki and Grizzle nodded.

As they were bowing out of the throne room, there was a commotion at the end of the corridor. They stepped quickly aside, as a host of guards bustled past with two prisoners. Nikki was shocked at the appearance of the guards – huge pigs with tusks, dressed in armour, walking on their hind legs. 'What's going on?' she asked Grizzle.

'I don't know, but they have Maleaver's son Lucan and Princess Gabriella.'

Maleaver was furious. Neither Gabriella nor Lucan had ever seen him in such a rage. His fury was directed mainly at his son.

'You were trying to escape with her? You are my son! Where is your loyalty? You will obey me! If you won't do it willingly then I will have to keep you under lock and key. Guards – take them to the tower and lock them in separate rooms.'

'You can't force us to get married!' Gabriella shouted as she was dragged away.

'I can do anything I wish!' Maleaver roared. 'In two days time you will be married and the kingdom of Elysia will be within my grasp.'

Chapter 7

Melusina

The rescue party followed the river all day, getting to know Fychan as they went. Ellie kept the map in front of her and could now see where they were. She thought that they had crossed into Morteribus. By sunset, they were on the lookout for a place to camp for the night. However, up ahead of them they saw a large house, set back a little way from the river, with a garden running down to the river. This seemed very unusual, as they had not passed any houses for some hours. Lucy, who had not been looking forward to another cold night out in the open, pleaded with the others to go and ask if they could stay the night. It was dark now, apart from a ghostly full moon, lighting their way. The fairies were enjoying the strengthening power of the moonlight and the girls remembered how much the moon had helped Gabriella to recover her magical powers. This made them all the more anxious to see her.

'Lucy, I'm not sure it's a good idea,' Ellie said. 'What if the person who lives there is not friendly? It seems a strange place to have a grand house like that – so close to Maleaver's castle. Remember, we are in his kingdom now.'

The others were in agreement with Ellie, so Lucy had to give in. Fychan, however, was curious, so when the others started to make camp he tiptoed away to check out the house. He decided not to approach from the front, but to pay a surprise visit by way of the river. He waded into the river and then began to swim as the water got deeper. He was enjoying his moonlit swim, when all of a sudden he stopped. Something as large as himself was shimmering in the moonlight, as it swam in the river just ahead of him. The creature appeared to be a large fish at first, but Fychan couldn't think of anything that was this big. Could it be another water nymph like himself? He thought not, as water nymphs wouldn't be living in Morteribus. Also, this creature definitely had a tail. He swam a little closer, silently slipping through the water. As he drew nearer, the fish-like creature did something impossible for a fish. It swam to the shore, where there was a little platform at the end of the garden, and wriggled out of the water. As Fychan watched, it was not a fish that emerged, but a woman: A woman with a fish's tail.

'A mermaid!' he gasped.

As the woman heaved her heavy jade coloured tail out of the water something even more remarkable happened: The tail turned to legs! She stood up and wrapped a robe around her. This was not even a mermaid. Mermaids did not have legs. Fychan was so surprised that he made a splashing noise.

'Who's there?' said the woman, peering back into the river.

Fychan was tempted to swim away quickly, but she said, 'Whoever you are, show yourself.' Her voice was commanding, but sweet, and flowed into Fychan's ear like a soothing lullaby. Slowly he emerged from the water and walked towards her. She was beautiful, with long auburn hair and smiling eyes.

'Who are you?' she said, as if finding a stranger swimming in her river at night was not even a little frightening.

'My name is Fychan, my lady,' he said, kneeling before her as if she were a queen.

'She laughed – a pretty tinkling laugh, like wind chimes hanging from a tree. 'Fychan. Please don't bow to me. You are a water nymph, I see. My name is Melusina. I am also a creature of the water, as you will have noticed, but I am part human too.'

'How can that be?' Fychan said, as she helped him to stand up.

'It is a long story. But may I ask why you were... spying on me?'

Fychan blushed and hesitated, but already he sensed that Melusina was someone he could trust. 'I'm sorry my lady. I have some friends – fairies and... humans. We need a place to stay for the night. We weren't sure if someone living in Morteribus would help us.'

'I understand,' she said. 'How many friends do you have with you?'

'There are five of us altogether.'

'You are welcome to stay with me. It is a while since I have had the pleasant company of fairy folk. And humans? That is very unusual. Would you like to bring your friends up to the house? I will go ahead and prepare some supper for you.'

'You're very kind, my lady.' Fychan headed back to bring the others.

The front door was open as they approached. Ellie was still very wary, despite Fychan's enthusiasm. She remembered how, on their first visit, Silveria had seemed so lovely at first, but then betrayed them to Grizzle.

'Welcome friends,' Melusina said, coming to greet them in a long, swaying, turquoise dress.

'Good evening,' Acantha said, taking charge. 'It is most kind of you to take us in tonight.'

There was a chorus of thank-yous.

'Come,' said Melusina, 'let's go into my living room by the fire. I've set out some supper.'

The room was large and grand, but had a cosiness about it with big plush armchairs and sofas around the blazing fire. Lucy was beaming by this time. They introduced themselves, but didn't share anything about their mission. Melusina understood their caution and didn't ask questions.

'It isn't often I get visitors. I'm glad you stopped by,' Melusina said.

'We are glad of somewhere warm to stay,' said Lucy. 'We've travelled a long way.'

'Indeed you have,' Melusina smiled. 'From the human world, I believe.' Lucy reddened as if it were supposed to be a secret. 'Did Fychan not tell you that I am part human too?'

'Yes,' said Lucy.

'Then you must know I would recognise another human? Even if Fychan hadn't already told me about you,' she said, smiling at Fychan.

Ellie scowled at him. 'If you don't mind me asking, why are you living here in Morteribus, especially if you are part human?'

Melusina's face clouded over and it was her turn to hesitate. Eventually she said, 'A long time ago I used to live at the castle...'

'Maleaver's castle?' Ellie asked, suddenly more on guard.

'Yes. I was fully human then. But Maleaver has a rather bad temper...'

'We know,' said Lucy, who was promptly elbowed in the ribs by Ellie.

'And he threw me out, making me into a half fish. He did give me this house, but I am banished from ever returning to the castle.'

'Why would you want to?' Adalira said.

'I have my reasons,' Melusina replied, but she was not about to reveal them. 'So, you have come across Maleaver before?' She looked at Lucy, who wished she had kept her big mouth shut.

'Yes, we've been to the castle before,' Lucy said, looking sheepishly at Ellie.

Ellie frowned. They had already said too much. But the fairies and Fychan seemed to be more trusting of their host.

'We are on our way there now, as a matter of fact,' Adalira said.

'Adalira!' Ellie exclaimed.

Adalira gave Ellie a scowl and continued. 'We need to get into the castle. You see, Queen Hermia of Elysia sent us to rescue her daughter, the Princess Gabriella.'

'I know of Elysia and the Queen,' said Melusina.

'Maleaver kidnapped the princess and now he is going to marry her to his son, in order to take power of Elysia,' Acantha continued.

'His son? You mean Lucan?' Melusina asked.

'Yes. We have to get in before it happens. We hope we're not already too late,' Acantha said.

'Poor Gabriella, she must be terrified and wondering if help will ever come,' Lucy said.

Melusina seemed not to be listening anymore. She had a faraway look on her face.

'If you don't mind,' Acantha said, 'Could we go to bed now? We are very tired and a good night's sleep will make the last part of our journey a little easier tomorrow.'

'Yes, of course,' Melusina said. 'But how about if I help you get into the castle tomorrow?'

'How could you do that?' asked Ellie.

'This river forks, up ahead, and one fork flows through the castle by way of an underground stream.

If you will permit me I can change you all into fish for a short time in the moonlight. You could swim in unnoticed. The magic would wear off after an hour though. I only have limited powers.'

'That would be amazing!' Fychan said.

The fairies and the girls were a little less enthusiastic about being turned into fish.

'What about our things? My lyre and Fychan's bow – we might need them,' Adalira said.

'I will turn you into large fish and we will tie them up in a bundle and harness them to one of you,' Melusina said.

'Won't that look very strange?' Ellie asked.

'We could use fairy magic to make them very small, so that they will not be noticed. We're very grateful to you,' Acantha said.

'Now, let me show you to your rooms.' Melusina led the way to several impressive bedrooms. 'Sleep well.'

Ellie and Lucy were sharing a room. 'What do you think of her?' Ellie whispered, as they lay together in a large four poster bed, in the dark. 'Lucy?' But Lucy was already asleep. Ellie shrugged and closed her eyes too.

As Melusina cleared away the food and prepared to go to bed herself, there was a loud banging on the door. She hoped it wouldn't wake her guests. This was turning out to be a busy night. She opened the oak door to find a party of goblins on the doorstep. The chief goblin came into the light, and she recognised him at once as Grizzle. But what shocked her was the appearance of another human girl, standing alongside him, with her arms folded across her chest and a frown on her face.

'Grizzle. It has been a long time since we last met. What can I do for you?' Melusina asked.

'Have you seen any humans in these parts recently?' he said.

'Humans? Of course not! I rarely see anyone and humans are the rarest of creatures in these parts. However, I see *you* have one,' she nodded at Nikki. 'Have you lost some others?'

Nikki stepped forward. Her expression suddenly changed to that of a lost puppy. 'They are my friends. Their names are Ellie and Lucy. I need to find them so we can go home together. Grizzle has said he will help us.'

'Has he now?' Melusina said, raising her eyebrows at Grizzle.

Grizzle knew that Melusina would never believe this and pushed Nikki back impatiently. 'Well, have you seen them? We may need to search your house.'

'You will do no such thing!' Melusina said, in a suddenly commanding tone. 'As I said, I have not seen anyone recently. I prefer my own company. Now, if that is all – goodnight to you!'

She cast one last curious look at Nikki and slammed the door. As she turned she saw Ellie and Lucy huddled at the top of the wide staircase. They had heard almost the whole conversation.

'They woke you,' she said. 'Sorry about that. A nuisance, but they will leave now.'

'How can you be sure?' Ellie asked.

'Because Grizzle has always been a coward. He's afraid of me,' she laughed.

'Thank you for not giving us away,' Ellie said.

'Do you know that girl who is with Grizzle?'

'Yes,' Lucy said. 'She followed us to the Fairy World and somehow ended up with Grizzle.'

'She's a bully at our school,' Ellie said.

'She is in great danger,' Melusina said.

Ellie and Lucy looked at each other. They hadn't talked about it much, but despite Nikki having bullied Lucy, they were both wondering what they should do about her.

Melusina smiled. 'You can't do anything about it tonight. Go back to bed, dear children. Goodnight.'

Gabriella awoke, back in her tower room. She was so down hearted that she didn't even want to get out of bed. She knew that tomorrow she would be forced to marry Lucan. Elysia was in grave danger. Tears from the night before had dried on her pillow and now fresh ones fell on top of them.

'Oh Mother, Father, why aren't you coming for me? And Ellie and Lucy – if only you were here.'

She rose from her bed and went to the window. From this high point she could see much of the castle and grounds. There were a lot of people scurrying about like mice below her. She realised that much of the activity was to do with preparations for the wedding tomorrow. Her heart sank even further and she lifted her eyes from the courtyard to look further afield, hoping that someone might be preparing to rescue her at this very minute.

Meanwhile, in another locked room in the tower, Maleaver was giving Lucan orders.

'You will be loyal to me – your father. You will treat the princess as I see fit and will not be kind to her. She needs to learn to obey you, otherwise you will have a problem on your hands. And you need to learn to obey me. Because if you don't, I will imprison you in a dark place forever! You are **my** son – so act like it!'

Lucan cowered away from his father's rage. He did not want to end up in a dark prison forever. At least here in the castle he had some freedom and that seemed like the best he was ever going to get. He had been foolish to try to help Gabriella and to think that they could escape from his powerful father. He had no choice: Though it may be cowardly, he would have to obey Maleaver.

'I am going to send you back to the princess today. You had better show me that you can obey me! I will have a servant in the room at all times, who will report back to me what he sees.'

When the door to her room opened, Gabriella was surprised and pleased to see Lucan. She ran to hug him. However, Lucan shrugged her off. 'Leave me alone! My father has sent me to teach you how to behave towards me.'

Gabriella backed away from him. Suddenly this was not the boy she had come to know as her friend anymore. Here was Maleaver's true son. 'But Lucan, you can't give in to him so easily. Remember all we have talked about. You are not like him.'

'Well maybe I should have been more like him all along,' Lucan barked. 'I will be more successful and powerful. After all, your kingdom will be mine, won't it. I will be ruler of Elysia.' He tried to sound like Maleaver.

Gabriella shuddered. 'Lucan, please – don't do this.'

'I am doing it. I've made up my mind. So you'd better get used to it Princess.'

Gabriella sank down onto the window seat and turned away from him. Everything felt hopeless now.

Nikki was fed up with Grizzle. He had done nothing but moan and grumble at her. He was treating her like his personal slave – get this, fetch that, cook this, get rid of that! To make matters worse, they had seen no signs of Ellie and Lucy. In less than one day they would have to return to the castle. And Nikki dreaded what would be waiting for them if they returned empty handed. She wondered if she should try to make a run for it. But the goblins kept a close watch on her, as if she was already their prisoner. Besides, where would she go? More than ever, she wished she was back home. Where were Lucy and Ellie? At this moment she thought she would actually be glad to see their familiar faces.

Grizzle drove them on without stopping. He was desperate to find the girls. He knew they were his only chance with Maleaver. This made him even more grumpy than usual. And although he appeared to be in charge of the other goblins, he knew that they had their orders if he failed to find Ellie and Lucy.

The rescue party was preparing to set off from Melusina's house. 'I wish I could change you into fish now and you could swim all the way. It would be safer. But my magic won't last long enough.'

'And our magic can't be used to turn people into animals,' said Adalira.

'We will have to walk as close to the castle as possible. Then, as the moon shows herself, I will turn you into fish. We must take great care. Grizzle and his goblins are roaming the countryside looking for you. They know you are not far away.'

'Before we go, Ellie, you need to sing your song to my lyre. If I need to use it, in the castle, I don't want you falling under its spell again,' Adalira said.

Ellie had dreaded this moment. 'Can I do it somewhere...private?' she asked.

Adalira took her to another room and placed the lyre before her.

'I don't know what to sing,' Ellie said. 'And I can't sing very well either.'

'Don't worry about that,' Adalira said. 'Just think about something you really love and make up some words about it and a tune to go with it. It doesn't have to be really tuneful. I'll leave you to it.'

Ellie sat for ages trying to think of something. She loved football and could think of lots of football chants, but this had to be her own unique song. She thought about her school team – about her friends Tom and Rhys and all the goals she'd saved. Some words began to come to her. 'Oh well, here goes,' she said to herself. She began to form a tune and hesitantly she sang her football song to the lyre. When she had finished she breathed a sigh of relief. As if in thanks, the lyre tinkled a little tune back to her, making Ellie jump.

Fychan had been sent out to see that there was no one watching the house. He was easily able to blend himself into the surrounding trees and bushes, like a chameleon. Finally, all was prepared and the rescue party set out. Everyone was nervous and there wasn't much talking as they kept a wary look out for the goblins.

When they came to the fork in the river, Lucy could see Maleaver's castle looming, like a fearful monster from a nightmare. She reached for Ellie's hand.

'Don't worry Lucy. Remember how brave you were last time,' Ellie said.

'But Perizam and Gabriella were with us then,' Lucy replied.

'And now we have Acantha, Adalira and Fychan. We can do it. Remember our saying – Together. Whatever!'

As the rescue party stood at the fork in the river, Grizzle and his party were only a mile or so behind them. It was nearly midnight and Grizzle was frantic. They had scanned the countryside for miles and found nothing. Now they were heading back towards the castle, because Grizzle's last hope was that they would find them trying to get in.

When the moon finally sailed out from behind the clouds, Melusina said, 'It's time. Are you ready?'

Everyone nodded. Fychan was excited at the thought of becoming a fish, whereas Ellie, Lucy and the fairies were very nervous.

'Don't worry,' Melusina said, smiling. 'You will be fine. Just swim hard and you will be into the castle in plenty of time, before the magic wears off. Fychan, you swim at the back to make sure everyone is okay. Now I have a request for you.' Melusina looked very serious.

'I wish I could come with you, but an enchantment prevents me from going any nearer to the castle. Inside that castle is something very precious to me and I would like you to find out as much as you can and bring me news.'

'Yes, of course,' Acantha said. 'We will do our best.'

'What is it?' Ellie asked.

'My son,' Melusina replied. 'Lucan is my son.'

No one knew what to say.

'I'm sure Maleaver has trained him to be like himself, but I would just like to know if he is well and what he looks like,' Melusina continued. 'I haven't seen him since he was a small child. That is when Maleaver threw me out. He didn't want Lucan to know who I was.'

'We will tell you all that we find out,' Acantha said, placing a hand on Melusina's arm.

'Do not tell him about me. He thinks I am dead and that is probably for the best. Now you must get into the river. You fairies, lift up your wings.'

'Wait, I need to make the bundle smaller,' Acantha said. She sprinkled dust on their belongings and the bundle shrank until it was the size of a nut to them. Melusina picked it up. 'I will attach this to you, Fychan, when you are a fish. You are bound to be the strongest swimmer.'

The water felt icy cold as they waded into it. Everyone but Fychan drew in their breath sharply.

'Don't be afraid,' Melusina reassured them. 'Now take a deep breath and hold it.'

Lucy and Ellie's hearts were pounding. They reached for each other's hands and squeezed.

'Remember...' Ellie said.

'Together. Whatever!' Lucy finished off, trying to smile.

Melusina began to chant some magical words and suddenly the people in front of her were gone. She looked down to see five silvery fish wiggling in the water. One splashed and dived – it was Fychan. Gently she coaxed him to her and fastened the bundle to his slippery tail.

'Swim now,' she said, and they glided away through the moonlit waters towards the castle. Melusina walked into the river. Her legs turned into the beautiful jade coloured tail.

At that moment Grizzle, Nikki and the goblins came into view. Melusina slipped gracefully under the water and swam back towards her house.

'What was that?' Nikki said, as a huge fish-like creature swam swiftly past her.

Grizzle looked into the river to see the tail of Melusina disappearing up stream.

'Melusina!' he cried. 'I knew she was up to something. Search this area thoroughly – they can't be far away.'

Chapter 8

Invasion

Five silvery fish, glinting in the bright moonlight, swam under the walls of Maleaver's castle, unnoticed. The stream flowed, dark and cold, for some way, under the castle. Even Ellie felt a little frightened. They were all glad when, finally, it opened out into a cellar and there was some light from burning brands, placed around the walls. These lit the way for servants coming down to collect wine, as well as water from the stream. Here the five fish stopped swimming ahead and began to swim around in circles and figures of eight, as if playing a game, when really they were waiting, in hope that the magic was going to wear off. None of them, even Fychan, liked the thought of remaining a fish forever.

It seemed like they swam round and round for a long time until they began to feel strange. A tingling began in their tails and an urge to breathe air began in their bellies. All at once the fish were no more and in their place, coughing and spluttering, sat the five friends.

'My wings!' exclaimed Adalira, standing up quickly. Acantha jumped up too.

'Don't worry,' Ellie said, looking at her hands as she lifted them out of the water. 'Look, we're not even wet.'

Everyone was standing up now, marvelling at how dry they were. 'I like this magic,' Acantha said.

They brought their parcel out of the water and, magically, it grew to its normal size. Fychan took out his bow and arrows, as Adalira took out her lyre. Examining their surroundings more closely, they could not tell what time it was down here, but they knew that it must still be night time. It took them a while to agree on a plan.

'I think we should split up and try to find Gabriella,' Ellie said. 'Perhaps we could meet back here by midday to find out how we've all got on. Hopefully we will have found her by then and can think of a way out.'

'Remember we have to find out about Lucan for Melusina – we owe her that, for her help,' Acantha reminded them.

'Yes, but our first duty is to get Gabriella to safety,' Lucy said.

'Maybe Ellie and I should stick together,' Lucy suggested, feeling the need to not be separated from her friend.

'Okay, but one of us should be with you, in case you need some magic,' Adalira said.

'I wouldn't count on your magic working here,' Ellie said. 'I think, after last time we were here, Maleaver will have found a way to stop any fairy magic in his castle.'

'Even so,' Acantha insisted, 'We can't leave you unprotected. Fychan, you go with them.'

'Of course,' Fychan said. 'It would be an honour to protect Ellie and Lucy. Although if Lucy had her own bow she wouldn't need protecting.'

Lucy grinned at him. 'And Ellie is an expert in karate,' she added.

'Right,' Acantha said, taking charge, 'let's head out of here. If anything happens to one party and the other party has the princess, you must not wait for the others. Just get the princess out of here. Understood?'

Everyone nodded. Ellie had the sudden urge to salute Acantha and this made her want to giggle.

At the top of the stone staircase, leading out of the cellar, was an arched wooden door. It had no windows in it, so they couldn't see if anyone was outside. Cautiously, Fychan turned the heavy metal ring that was the handle. It creaked and groaned, as the door opened outwards. Cringing, Fychan peered around the door. The corridor was clear, so they all moved out. It was a dark passageway, except for the burning torches. Silently, the two parties said goodbye to each other. Ellie, Lucy and Fychan went left, and Adalira and Acantha turned right.

Ellie's group soon found themselves at the foot of another staircase. The corridor continued beyond the staircase, but Ellie motioned for them all to go up. The other two nodded. Fychan insisted on going first. At the top of the stairs was another corridor, this time with many doors leading off it. So far, they had encountered no one and heard no noise. Most people must be asleep. However, as they moved along this corridor they came to a door, behind which there was a lot of activity: Clanging, banging, chopping, shouting.

'Kitchen,' Lucy whispered.

'But why are they so busy in the middle of the night?' Ellie said.

'They're probably preparing for the wedding. What if it is tomorrow – or today even?' said Lucy, thinking it must be past midnight.

'Come on,' Fychan said, motioning for them to follow him.

They continued along the corridor until they came to some windows. These were arched, with criss-cross patterns across the coloured glass. Suddenly, several figures passed close by, outside. Fychan and the girls ducked down. They could hear gruff voices and, if Ellie wasn't mistaken, a girl crying. Immediately, she thought of Gabriella. So did Lucy, who had to put her hand to her mouth to stifle a gasp.

'We have to find out where they're taking her,' Ellie said.

Fychan motioned them to follow him. Keeping low beneath the windows, they found a door that led outside. They could still hear the tramping of heavy feet, but it seemed further away. Pressing themselves into the shadows along the wall, Ellie, Lucy and Fychan crept through the courtyard, following the sound of the voices. A violet tinge was seeping into the inky black sky: A sign that dawn was not far off. Up ahead,

they could see a shadowy group of creatures that Ellie and Lucy immediately recognised as Maleaver's pig-like guards. They had their backs to Ellie, Lucy and Fychan, but seemed to be guarding prisoners. The three stopped to listen, as a guard came out of a door and began to speak.

'Lord Maleaver is preparing to see you. Your snivelling excuses won't make any difference now,' he grunted. The other guards laughed. The sound of crying, which had faded to a whimper, began again in earnest.

'And you can shut up! Lord Maleaver hates crying snivelling girls!'

Lucy wished she could see past the bulky guards. She wanted to catch a glimpse of Gabriella and possibly Lucan. What was going on?

Then the crying voice piped up. 'It's not fair! This is not my fault. I was only trying to help! What are you going to do to us? I want to go home!'

At once Ellie and Lucy recognised the voice. This was not Gabriella – it was Nikki. Lucy almost gasped again.

Another voice came from inside the circle of guards. 'Oh, be quiet human! You are in as much trouble as I am. Lord Maleaver will no doubt have some horrible fate awaiting us. There's nothing you can do about it, so you might as well save your breath.'

It was Grizzle! Grizzle and Nikki!

'I want to go home,' Nikki wailed. 'I'm not supposed to be here. It's all their fault – Ellie and Lucy. I never wanted to come here. I want to go...'

'Shut up!' chorused the guards and Grizzle together. The shock made Nikki stop.

'Come on, let's get them inside. Lord Maleaver will be waiting,' said the guard.

'We have to help her!' Lucy whispered.

'Who is she?' Fychan asked.

'She is a bully from our school, who somehow followed us here. She has been helping Grizzle to try and find us, to hand us over to Maleaver,' Ellie said.

'So leave her to her fate,' Fychan said. 'Sounds to me like she deserves it!'

'We can't!' Lucy protested. 'Ellie, we just can't leave her here. She doesn't belong here.'

'Lucy, she was horrible to you at school and even here she has tried to get us caught by Grizzle and handed over to Maleaver.'

'I know, but she doesn't know what she's doing. No one deserves to face Maleaver's punishments.'

Ellie frowned. A part of her wanted to see Nikki Walters get what she deserved. As if reading her thoughts Lucy said, 'I know she's been horrible to us but she doesn't really deserve this.'

'We need to find Gabriella first,' Ellie said.

'I agree,' Fychan said.

'But what if Maleaver is turning her into something horrible at this very moment?' Lucy said.

'There's not much we can do about it then,' Fychan said.

'Please Ellie, we have to try,' Lucy said.

'Okay, after we've found Gabriella,' Ellie said.

As they crept along the wall, the door, through which the guards had taken Nikki and Grizzle, opened. The three friends leapt back behind some barrels. They were bringing Nikki and Grizzle out.

'Get them in the dungeons,' the guard barked. 'Lord Maleaver is going to have fun turning you into little ornaments as wedding gifts – right before the very eyes of the bride and groom. Only a few hours to wait. ' All the guards laughed as Nikki and Grizzle were pushed and shoved towards the door to the dungeons.

'Only a few hours to the wedding!' Lucy whispered when the courtyard had fallen silent again. 'We've got to help Nikki.'

'The princess comes first,' Fychan insisted. 'And what about Grizzle? How are you going to get her out without Grizzle?'

'Wait,' Ellie said. 'I've had an idea. Come on, we're going to get into those dungeons again, Lucy.'

'Ellie!' Fychan said.

'Trust me, Fychan. Come on.'

Chapter 9

Search

Ellie and Lucy knew the way to the dungeons from their last visit to Maleaver's castle, but they had to acquire some keys somehow. They watched as two guards came back from locking Grizzle and Nikki in the dungeon. They pulled the heavy door, at the top of the steps, closed behind them and locked it with a large bunch of keys. Then they made their way to a bench nearby and slumped heavily onto it against the wall. They spent several minutes arguing over who would keep first watch while the other had a snooze. In the end they both decided it would be fine to drop off and it wasn't long before they were snoring.

'We're going to free Grizzle and Nikki,' Ellie said. 'But we need those keys. Can you get them, Fychan?'

Fychan hopped restlessly from one foot to the other. 'Yes. Easy. But why? Is this going to help us find the princess?'

'I'm hoping so,' Ellie said. 'Now, can you get those keys?'

Fychan flitted across the courtyard. The sky was now a pale grey, but he was swift and had amazing ways of camouflaging himself against objects and in shadows. He reminded Lucy of Peter Pan. As if he was a shadow himself, he silently picked the keys from the guard's belt and made his way towards the dungeon door. Ellie and Lucy came out of their hiding place and followed him. More people were starting to come and go across the courtyard and Lucy was sure they would be spotted at any moment. They crouched behind some crates near the dungeon door. In the few moments when the coast was clear, they darted out and Fychan managed to unlock the door.

There were many steps down to the dungeons and once again it was dark, apart from burning torches along the walls. It smelled damp and Lucy felt goose bumps appearing on her skin. Ellie and Lucy knew from last time that there would be no guards down here. They were supposed to guard at the top, but they clearly didn't take this too seriously. When they finally reached the bottom of the stairs they came to a large dark chamber. Around the outside of the chamber were caves with bars in front of them. Cautiously, Ellie, Lucy and Fychan peered into each one. The caves were like black holes, without any torches inside them. There were one or two other prisoners, but no one took any notice of them. They were beginning to wonder if Nikki and Grizzle were actually here, when Grizzle came up to the bars of the last cave. He was shocked to see them.

'What are you doing here? The princess is not down here. You don't think Lord Maleaver would keep her locked up here before her wedding do you?'

'Where's Nikki?' Ellie demanded.

Nikki had heard Ellie's voice and rushed to the front of the cave. She looked at Ellie and Lucy as if they were her long-lost best friends.

'Get me out of here! How did you get in? Can you get me out?' she cried, panic rising in her voice.

'You don't deserve to be let out from what I hear,' Fychan said.

'Ellie – please! I want to go home,' Nikki pleaded, ignoring Fychan.

'We can get you out – both of you, but we need your help to get Princess Gabriella out of the castle,' Ellie said.

'If you promise to help us, we will set you free,' Lucy said.

Fychan held up the keys, somewhat reluctantly.

'Grizzle,' Ellie said. 'You've got nothing to lose, if you help us. Maleaver has turned against you. If you won't help us, then we'll leave you in Maleaver's hands.'

'What about me?' Nikki wailed.

'You have to do as Ellie tells you,' Lucy said.

'I will. I'll do anything to get home,' Nikki said, pressing her face against the bars. Even in this light Lucy could see tear streaks in the grime on her face. Even Ellie felt sorry for her. She looked so helpless.

'And what about you?' Fychan said to Grizzle. 'Will you do as Ellie says?'

'A chance of freedom has to be worth doing a human's bidding for a short time,' Grizzle said, grudgingly.

'When we release you, I want you to help us find the princess. You know this castle much better than any of us Grizzle. Then, you help us to find our friends and get out of here. You must know secret ways out of here.'

'It seems like a risky plan,' Grizzle said.

'It is, but it's all I can think of, if we're going to be able to help Nikki here,' Ellie said.

'Oh please, just get me out of here,' Nikki cried.

'Are you sure about this? These two don't seem very trustworthy to me,' Fychan said.

'Come on,' said Lucy. 'Let's do it before we change our minds.' She took the keys from Fychan and they worked their way through the bunch, until they found the one to unlock the cave.

Nikki nearly hugged Lucy, then thought better of it. Lucy looked at this big year six girl, who had bullied her and frightened her many times in the past, and she wasn't at all scared of her any more. She felt sorry for her.

They hurried to the top of the stairs and looked out through the grill in the door. The courtyard was a bustle of activity and excitement. They could hear people talking about the wedding that was about to take place in just a few hours. Ellie hoped the others had already found Gabriella and were on their way back to the cellar.

Adalira and Acantha had indeed found the tower where Gabriella and Lucan were being held in separate rooms. They had overheard servants talking as they went to and fro from the tower, with all sorts of things, to prepare Gabriella and Lucan for the wedding ceremony.

'I think we should disguise ourselves as servants to get into the room where the princess is being held,' said Acantha.

'Good idea,' Adalira agreed. 'I could try sending a couple of them to sleep next time they come by and we could use their clothes.'

'I hope the lyre works,' Acantha said. 'Remember what Ellie said about Maleaver being able to stop fairy magic.'

'I know, but the lyre works differently to ordinary fairy magic,' Adalira said. 'Look, here come a couple of servants now. Let's try it.'

The servants were carrying the bridal dress between them. It was beautiful: White, with tiny pearls sewn in intricate patterns all over it. They were struggling to keep it from trailing on the ground. As the servants came near to where the fairies were hiding, Adalira began to play one of the lyre's sleep-making tunes. The two servants looked around to see where the music was coming from.

'It's not going to work,' Acantha whispered. However, as they watched, the servants began to teeter around and then both fell to the floor, dropping the dress they were carrying.

Quickly, the two fairies darted out and heaved the two servants into their hiding place. Acantha tried some magic to pull them along but, as predicted, it didn't work. The fairies put the servants' clothing over their own and tucked their wings into the back of the outfits. One of the servants had a bunch of keys, which Acantha took from her. Then, they picked up the heavy dress and Adalira tucked her lyre underneath its folds.

'I hope it hasn't got dirty,' Adalira said, examining the dress.

'That's not important, is it?' Acantha said, sounding rather like a headmistress. 'Come on, we've got to get to the princess.'

They made their way up the stairs in the tower, but they were uncertain where to start looking for Gabriella. There were several different floors leading off the staircase.

'Let's go right to the top and work our way down,' said Acantha. 'If I were keeping an important prisoner, I'd keep them at the top.'

Suddenly, a woman's voice called out to them from above. 'Hurry up with that dress! Where have you been? We've been waiting for ages!'

'I guess we've found her,' Adalira said, feeling excited all of a sudden. 'I hope they don't get suspicious that we're not those other two.'

The woman was waiting for them at the top of the stairs. She did look at them strangely. 'What happened to Agnes and Bea?'

'Oh didn't they tell you? We're from the dressmaker's and we wanted to come and do the final fitting ourselves,' said Adalira, hoping that her bluff would work. 'Those two servants have been sent to do something else.'

The woman gave her another strange look.

'My! Your preparations are going well,' Acantha said. 'The castle is looking splendid. It's going to be a marvellous wedding isn't it? Now, where is the bride?'

Enjoying the praise, the woman, who was very excited about the wedding, forgot her suspicions. 'Yes, it is very exciting,' she said. 'We haven't had a wedding here since... well since Lord Maleaver himself got married, but we don't really talk about that anymore. Yes, this will give the place a new lease of life.' She ushered the supposed dressmakers into the room.

Gabriella was standing in the middle of the room in a silk dressing gown. Her hair was tied back in a beautiful arrangement, scattered with tiny pearls, and delicate strands of hair curling down from the sides. She was surrounded by several other women who were fussing over her. But unlike most brides on their wedding day, Gabriella's face was a picture of unhappiness. Adalira and Acantha were shocked to see their princess looking so sad.

As soon as Gabriella saw them, she recognised them. They saw it in her eyes and the tiny flicker of a smile that passed across her face.

'Good morning to you, Princess,' said Acantha. 'We are here from the dressmaker's, to fit you into this marvellous gown. Only our finest for a princess. It is our honour to serve you.' The fairies bowed low before Gabriella.

'Thank you,' she said. 'I'm most grateful that you have come in person.'

'Oh we wouldn't have it any other way,' Adalira said.

'Now, if the rest of you would leave us for a while, we would like to fit this dress without an audience. Then you will all be amazed when you see the princess appear with it on.'

The other servants looked at each other; some in annoyance, others not sure what they should do, as they had been told not to leave the princess unattended.

'Come now,' Acantha said, clapping her hands at them. 'This won't take long.'

The woman who had shown them in, began to usher the other servants out of the room. 'Come along everyone, I'll call you back shortly. Don't go far.' She was obviously in charge and planned to stay in the room herself.

'You too, if you don't mind,' said Acantha in her most jolly voice. 'We want to surprise you all!'

The woman looked irritated, but left the room, locking the door behind her.

Gabriella rushed to the fairies. 'Oh, Adalira, Acantha – thank goodness you've come. I had given up hope! Is it just you?'

'No Princess, Fychan is here and Ellie and Lucy too,' said Adalira.

'Ellie and Lucy? They came! I hoped they would somehow.'

'Your mother sent them a message. Your father has been summoned back and will hopefully be on his way here with reinforcements as we speak,' said Acantha. 'I'm sorry it has taken so long to get here. We have had some problems along the away. But at least we're not too late.'

'What are we going to do now?' asked Gabriella.

'You will have to wear the wedding dress, so we don't arouse suspicion. Then, we're going to get you out of here,' Acantha said.

Chapter 10

The Wedding

When the courtyard was clear, Ellie and the others pushed open the door to the dungeon and slipped out, past the useless guards who were still sleeping on the bench.

'I have a feeling that the princess and Master Lucan will be in the North Tower. They tried to escape, apparently, so they will be under lock and key,' Grizzle said.

' Lucan tried to escape?' Ellie said.

'He was helping the princess. Fool!' Grizzle said.

Ellie wondered what they would do about Lucan. Melusina wanted news of him.

At that moment, a group of people came into view, carrying banqueting food from the kitchen. 'Get down!' Fychan urged. They crouched behind a stone water trough until the people had disappeared. But no sooner had they passed, than a band of musicians came laughing and joking across the courtyard, followed by jesters and other entertainers. After that, more people bustled to and fro.

'This is impossible!' said Ellie. 'Someone is going to see us soon. We need to move somewhere else.'

'Come on,' Grizzle said. 'After this next lot have disappeared we're going to make a run for that door over there.' He pointed ahead of them to the left. 'That will take us through several corridors to the North Tower.'

They watched the last person disappear round a corner. 'Now!' Fychan called and they ran to the door, almost falling inside.

Lucy thought that the corridor was not a main walkway, as there was no one around and it wasn't very grand. She felt a little relieved. Nikki was sticking close to her for some reason.

'Are you alright?' Lucy asked her. Nikki nodded, but her face was sweaty and her eyes wide. She didn't look alright. Lucy tried to smile at her.

'This way,' Grizzle said. 'Keep a look out for servants.'

The girls followed Grizzle, with Fychan bringing up the rear, his bow at the ready. They took several different turns and went through a few doors. Ellie found herself feeling grateful for Grizzle's guidance. They just hoped that Gabriella was in the North Tower. Grizzle stopped at a door that led outside.

'We have to cross this small courtyard and that door over there leads up to the tower.' He peered out of a window. Servants were going back and forth through the door at the foot of the tower, carrying various things.

'There's lots of activity, which means she is almost certainly in there,' Grizzle said.

'Good!' said Fychan. 'Let's get her out.'

'How? There are so many people,' Nikki said, speaking for the first time since leaving the dungeons.

'We will just have to wait for the right moment,' Ellie said.

After what seemed an age, the courtyard emptied. 'Now's our chance,' said Fychan. He pushed past Grizzle and opened the door. Ellie, Lucy and Nikki followed. Grizzle came last.

They hurried to the door of the North Tower.

'Stop!'

They turned to see several of Maleaver's guards behind them. They had not been able to see them from inside the corridor.

'Escaped prisoners!' shouted the guard. 'Get them!'

Fychan already had an arrow in his bow.

'You might as well put it down!' the guard ordered, laughing at Fychan. 'It will only bounce off my hard skin!'

Fychan fired.

'You see?' the guard said, as the arrow bounced off him. 'Now, arrest them!'

Grizzle, walked calmly towards the guards. 'Thank goodness you're here,' he said. 'These humans released me from the dungeons to help them, but I've been

looking for a place to secure them until I could come for you. I am loyal to the Lord Maleaver, as I have always been. Please let me present them to him.'

The guards looked Grizzle up and down. Then they took hold of the others. 'Let's see what he says, shall we?'

'Grizzle!' Ellie hissed, as she was being dragged away. 'How could you?'

Grizzle just smiled his goblin smile of crooked blackened teeth. Nikki began to cry again.

Maleaver was not pleased to be interrupted. He was preparing himself for the wedding.

'So Grizzle, you finally bring me the humans? Or did they bring you – I can't make up my mind.' He came up close to Ellie. 'So how did you get into my castle this time?'

Lucy and Nikki were trembling together. Ellie tried to stay calm, but her insides had turned to gloop and were sloshing about under her skin. She refused to speak to Maleaver. He laughed.

'I remember you; the bravest one!' Then he turned to Lucy. 'And another, trying to be brave.' Lucy tried not to let the tears, that were pricking the backs of her eyes, spill out. Then he turned to Nikki. 'And here we have a true coward, if ever I saw one.' Nikki dissolved into tears again. 'So Grizzle – ever loyal – through thick and thin, eh?'

'Yes my Lord,' Grizzle said, grovelling before Maleaver.

Maleaver sighed. 'Decisions, decisions... Turn you to stone now and get it done, or give you one more chance to prove yourself. Hmm...'

'I only want the chance to serve you again, Master.'

Maleaver smirked at Grizzle. 'Very well then, you pathetic little creature. It is my son's wedding day. I'm feeling... generous. Get yourself ready to join the celebrations in the banqueting hall, in fifteen minutes. Prove your loyalty.'

Grizzle backed out of the room muttering thank you after thank you.

'Creep!' Ellie shouted at him. Lucy bit back a smile, despite her fear.

'Generous... generous,' Maleaver was saying, almost to himself. 'Therefore, I will grant you the privilege of seeing the wedding, before I turn the three of you into ornaments for the princess and Lucan.' His voice began to get louder until he was shouting. 'Then you can be a constant reminder to them of what happens to people who cross me!'

All three girls cowered.

The servants in the North Tower marvelled at how beautiful Gabriella looked. Her fairy wings fluttered out behind her from the specially made dress. The woman in charge even had a tear in her eye. A messenger came to tell them that Maleaver and Lucan were waiting for Gabriella in the banqueting hall. The servants went ahead and Adalira and Acantha followed behind Gabriella.

'How can we get her away?' Adalira hissed, as they made their way down the stairs. 'Shall I play the lyre?'

'Not on the stairs,' Acantha whispered back, 'Someone could get hurt. Wait 'til we get into the courtyard.'

However, when they arrived in the courtyard, Gabriella was suddenly whisked away from them by footmen in wedding outfits. She glanced back at Acantha and Adalira. Hurriedly, Adalira began to play, but the woman in charge smacked Adalira's hands away from the lyre.

'No time for that!' she scolded. 'They've got to get the princess to the banqueting hall. She mustn't be late. You can come with us to the servants' place if you want to watch.'

'What do we do now?' Adalira asked, as they were carried along with the crowd of servants hurrying excitedly to take their places.

Lucan stood at the front of the banqueting hall, dressed in wedding finery, waiting nervously. This was it. When he married Gabriella he would become the powerful heir to two kingdoms – under his father's direction of course. The thought terrified him. And Gabriella would become no more than his servant, to do as he told her – or as his father ordered him to tell her. He thought fondly of Gabriella and made up his mind that he would be as kind to her as he could, whenever his father was not breathing down his neck.

Maleaver came to stand next to Lucan. 'So, are you ready to take power over Elysia?'

'Yes father,' Lucan said, without looking at him.

'Once we have the princess in our power, we will work on getting rid of her mother and father. Then, who knows which kingdom I will conquer next!'

Lucan looked up at his father. Maleaver's face was twisted into a hideous grin and, in that moment, Lucan realised how much he hated all this.

Guests were seated, and chattered excitedly in hushed voices. The castle had not seen anything as extravagant as this for a long time. The banqueting hall was decorated in garlands and flowers, giving the impression that this was a joyful celebration.

At the back of the hall, Adalira and Acantha strained to see what was going on at the front. 'Look!' Acantha whispered. She pointed to a couple of guards bringing prisoners into the hall. Ellie, Lucy, Fychan and Nikki were marched to the front. Silence fell, as guests stared at them. Maleaver nodded to the guards to place them where Gabriella would be able to see them. Ellie and Lucy got their first sight of Lucan.

From the servants' places, near the back of the hall, Acantha and Adalira watched the others being paraded to the front. 'How are we going to get out of this?' wailed Adalira. 'It's all gone wrong!'

'Hush!' Acantha said. 'We'll think of something!'

A fanfare drowned out any more conversation. Then every head turned, as Gabriella was led into the hall and processed down the middle of the room, in front of all the guests. A veil covered her face, and the only evidence that she was crying underneath it, was the shuddering movements of her shoulders and wings. People smiled and gasped, unaware of her unhappiness. As she came to a stop at the front, Lucan turned to look at her, but she did not look at him.

Gabriella lifted her head and, to her horror, she saw the prisoners, under guard, at the front.

'These are your wedding presents, Princess,' Maleaver whispered in her ear. 'I'm going to make them into little ornaments, for you to keep.'

Gabriella gasped and started to move towards Ellie and Lucy, but Maleaver stopped her. Then he took Lucan's hand and gripped it around hers.

'Hold on to her,' he said to Lucan. Lucan held her hand so tightly that it hurt. He wanted to say sorry, but he was too afraid of his father to speak.

'We have to do something!' Ellie said.

Fychan tried to launch himself forward, but he was grasped tightly by the guard.

Maleaver began by welcoming the guests and handing over to the official who would conduct the service. When it came to the part where Gabriella had to make her vows to Lucan, she refused.

'I won't marry him!' she protested loudly, much to Maleaver's annoyance.

A collective gasp echoed around the banqueting hall.

'You will say the vows!' Maleaver ordered.

'You can't make me, and so I will not be married to your son,' Gabriella said defiantly.

'If you don't...' Maleaver began.

'You will do something horrible to me! I know! Well I don't care. Do your worst. I will not give Elysia to you!'

There were murmurs among the guests. What would Maleaver do?

'Lucan, talk to her!' Maleaver commanded.

Lucan looked at Gabriella, then he released her hand. 'No father, I will not say the vows either.'

Maleaver's face turned a horrible shade of purple.

Chapter 11

Chaos

'You will not disobey me!' he bellowed. 'Both of you have tried my patience to the limit. I will take Elysia without you! Enough of this. He raised his hand and Ellie knew, in an instant, that he was about to throw powerful magic at Gabriella and Lucan. She made to run in front of them, but a guard grabbed her. Maleaver was distracted, for a moment, by Ellie's movement.

'Not this time!' he sneered at her, raising his hand again. Lucan tried to protect Gabriella.

But as Maleaver was about to strike, Nikki dodged away from the guards and flung herself between Maleaver and Gabriella. The magic hit her and she fell to the floor. There was a sudden commotion from the back and, to everyone's surprise, Grizzle rushed in followed by a host of goblins. They charged down the hall towards Maleaver.

'What is the meaning of this?' Maleaver cried.

Guards moved forward to intercept the goblins and Lucy and Ellie rushed to look after Nikki. Lucan pulled Gabriella out of the path of the charging goblins.

'Come on Gabriella,' he urged, seizing her hand and running into the crowd.

Nikki made a groaning sound.

'She's okay,' Lucy gasped.

'Come on, let's get out of here,' Ellie said.

Fychan had joined Grizzle and the goblins. Adalira and Acantha pushed their way through the crowds to get to Gabriella. The whole place was in an uproar now. Some of the guests were joining in the fighting, while others were pushing and shoving to get out of the way.

Ellie and Lucy helped Nikki up and followed Lucan and Gabriella.

'I'm so glad you came for me!' Gabriella cried.

'No time for thank yous now, 'Ellie said. 'This is our chance to escape. Come on.'

'What about the others?' said Lucy.

'They will find us. Our main task is to get Gabriella to safety.'

The goblins and Fychan were putting up a good fight, but Maleaver's guards started to overpower the goblins and Maleaver was sending thunderbolts of magic into their ranks, turning many to stone statues.

'Capture my son and the princess – and those humans!' he cried.

Acantha and Adalira were now in the middle of the hall. They had found Fychan and Acantha was putting her karate skills into practice. 'I think Ellie and Lucy have got out of here with the princess but we are being overpowered,' she said.

'Let me try the lyre,' Adalira said.

She pulled the instrument from her bag and began to play the tune that made everyone fall asleep. Gradually, the people around her began to fall to the ground. She moved through the crowd towards Maleaver's guards, playing the tune as loudly as she could, to be heard over the noise. Guards tried to seize the lyre, but she was quick and nimble and dodged out of their way, until they fell down around her.

'It's working,' Fychan shouted, ducking out of the way of another guard.

'Let's get out of here,' Acantha said.

'Not so fast, little fairies!' Maleaver towered over them. The lyre didn't have any effect on him and, in shock, Adalira dropped it. 'You've turned this wedding to chaos and for that you will be punished.'

'Stop!' Grizzle stood behind the towering figure.

Maleaver turned. 'Traitor!' he growled. Acantha, Adalira and Fychan took their chance and ran.

Maleaver raised his hand towards Grizzle. The goblin cowered to accept his fate, but, at that moment, there was a thunderous sound, and a tidal wave of fairies and woodland creatures burst into the hall, from every side.

'Maleaver, you are defeated! Surrender!' It was Prince Lysander.

'Never!' Maleaver shouted. There was a puff of smoke and he disappeared from sight.

'Prince Lysander,' cried Acantha, bowing before him.

'Where is my daughter?' he asked.

'She is with Ellie and Lucy. They are trying to get her to safety.'

'Find them,' Lysander ordered a couple of his men.

Grizzle was still cowering on the floor. 'Bring this one,' Lysander said to another man.

'He has helped us, sire,' Acantha said.

Lysander raised an eyebrow in surprise. 'Bring him anyway.'

'Thank you for all you have done,' Lysander said to Acantha, Fychan and Adalira.

'Ellie and Lucy rescued us and put us back on track to find the princess,' Fychan said.

'Let's go and find them then,' Lysander said.

Maleaver's guards and guests were being rounded up. Lysander made his way out of the hall, into the courtyard, followed by Acantha, Adalira and Fychan. To his delight, Gabriella was being brought towards him, accompanied by Ellie, Lucy, Nikki and Lucan. She ran into her father's arms and he hugged her tight.

Then he turned to Ellie and Lucy, with a beaming smile. 'My dear friends. You came back to help us. The Queen and I are grateful to you once again. And who is this?' he said indicating Nikki.

'She is our friend, Nikki Walters,' Lucy said.

'She saved Gabriella from Maleaver's spell,' Ellie added. She turned to Nikki and smiled.

'I am also in your debt, young lady,' Lysander said.

Nikki blushed. 'I didn't do anything, sir. It was really all down to Ellie and Lucy. They saved us all.'

'You were very brave Nikki,' Lucy said. 'It's your bravery that saved you from Maleaver's spell.'

'Human courage seems to act like a shield,' Ellie said.

For the first time ever, Ellie and Lucy saw Nikki smile.

Lysander turned to Lucan, who had remained silent with his head bowed. 'Are you married to my daughter?' he asked.

'No sir,' Lucan replied.

Lysander breathed a sigh of relief. 'Bring him with the goblin,' he said to his men.

'Father,' Gabriella said. 'Lucan is my friend. He has done much to help me and has put himself in danger, with his father, several times.'

Lysander turned to Lucan, in surprise. 'Indeed?' Lucan looked up at him. 'Then you are welcome in my kingdom and in my palace if you will come with us.'

'Please come, Lucan,' Gabriella said.

Everyone looked expectantly at Lucan.

He looked around at his father's castle, then back to Gabriella. 'I will come,' he said. 'Thank you.'

'Prince Lysander,' Ellie said, ' On the way back to Elysia, can we stop somewhere? It won't take very long, but we promised the person who helped us get into the castle that we would bring her some important news.'

'Of course Ellie,' Lysander said. 'You must keep your promise and I would like to thank her myself.'

The party set off, accompanied by many fairies and woodland creatures. Some rode on horses and unicorns, some rode in carriages, while others ran or flew. When Maleaver's castle was well behind them, Lucy dared to say, 'I wonder what happened to Maleaver.'

'He vanished before our eyes,' Adalira said.

'But I'm certain he'll be back,' Fychan added.

Gabriella was overjoyed to be reunited with her old friends, Ellie and Lucy. They hugged each other and talked non-stop about all sorts of things. Nikki felt slightly awkward and didn't say much, but Ellie and Lucy did their best to make her feel involved.

It wasn't long before Ellie spotted Melusina's house. 'This is where we should stop,' she said to Prince Lysander.

Most of the fairies and woodland creatures were sent on their way with many thanks. Only a few remained with Prince Lysander and the others. They knocked on the door. Lucy could hardly contain her excitement to see Melusina's reaction when she saw her son standing in front of her.

Melusina opened the door. 'Oh, you got out! And you came back!' she exclaimed. 'Where is the princess?'

Gabriella stepped forward. She was still in the wedding gown. Melusina curtsied. 'Please, come into my home. Do you have news of my son?' she asked Gabriella.

'We have more than just news,' Ellie said.

Lucan stepped forward. He couldn't quite believe what was happening. 'Mother?'

Melusina was overcome with emotion. She grasped Lucan by the arms, then touched his face with her fingers. 'Lucan? Is it really you?'

'It is. I thought you were... father told me...'

'I know. Come in – all of you.'

Melusina took the whole party into her house and made them welcome. With the help of Lucy and the fairies she rustled up a feast for everyone. She wanted to know all about the rescue and how they had taken to being fish! But most of all she wanted be with her son.

'We have so much catching up to do,' she said to Lucan.

Lucan turned to Gabriella. 'Would you mind if I stayed here with my mother for a while?'

'Of course not,' Gabriella said, smiling at him. 'This is where you should stay. Your home is here with Melusina.'

Before too long Prince Lysander wanted to get underway. Queen Hermia would be anxious to see Gabriella once the messengers told her the good news.

'I will come and visit you,' Lucan said to Gabriella.

'I hope so,' Gabriella smiled.

'Thank you so much for bringing my son back to me,' Melusina said, tears of joy flowing down her cheeks. ' I will never forget what you've done for me.'

'And I will not forget that you helped to save my daughter,' said Lysander, taking Melusina's hand and kissing it.

When the rescue party arrived back in Elysia, they knew they were expected. Flags and banners adorned the streets, as Prince Lysander led the small procession to the castle. Many fairies came out of their homes to cheer and welcome them. Ellie and Lucy heard their names called out many times. It was very strange being heroines again. They felt rather uncomfortable and Nikki wanted to hide. But Prince Lysander and Gabriella waved regally to the crowds.

As they arrived at the castle, a welcome party was waiting to greet them. They were ushered into the Queen's chambers, where Queen Hermia was waiting to receive them. Once she saw her daughter, she could contain her royal composure no longer and rushed to Gabriella, picking her up and twirling her in her arms. Lysander joined them and everyone watched quietly as the royal family were reunited.

After a while, the Queen turned to the others. 'My friends,' she said, holding out her arms to them. 'I have so much to thank you for. Acantha, Adalira, Fychan – yet again you have proved your bravery and skill. You are my most worthy subjects.' The three knelt before the Queen.

'Ellie and Lucy, you came. Thank you. Again you have saved the kingdom of Elysia. You are our most honoured friends and I can never thank you enough.' Ellie and Lucy knelt before the Queen too, but she motioned for them to stand and, much to their surprise, gave them a great big hug. Gabriella, laughing at their faces, came to join in.

'And who is this?' the Queen asked, turning to Nikki.

Nikki stood with her head bowed, afraid to look at the Queen.

'This is Nikki, your Majesty,' Lucy explained. 'She was once our enemy, but she has shown great courage in helping to rescue Gabriella and she's now our friend.'

'Come forward Nikki,' the Queen commanded.

As Nikki took timid steps towards Queen Hermia, the Queen grasped her hand and shook it firmly. 'Thank you. You are welcome in my kingdom.'

Nikki looked up. Queen Hermia smiled her warm radiant smile at her and Nikki realised that once again she was being accepted. A slow smile spread across her face and she curtsied to the Queen.

It was then that Prince Lysander summoned a guard to bring one more person forward. Grizzle entered the room, chained between two guards. Queen Hermia looked puzzled.

'This goblin helped us enormously in the last battle against Maleaver,' Prince Lysander said. 'But I'm still not sure where his loyalties lie.'

The Queen looked at Grizzle. He was bold enough to stare back at her. 'Can you tell us where your loyalties lie?' she asked.

'With myself,' Grizzle declared. 'However, if you will give me my freedom, I swear I will never lift a finger against you or your kingdom again.'

Prince Lysander and Queen Hermia looked at each other. 'We will consider your request. You helped to save my daughter. Whatever your reasons for doing it, I am grateful, ' said the Queen. 'But for now you will remain in our... care; under guard but in comfort.' The Queen indicated for the guard to take him away.

'There will be celebrations this evening,' the Queen said, smiling at everyone. 'Our servants will show you to your rooms so that you can prepare yourselves.'

Nikki was overwhelmed by the beauty of the fairy castle. As a little girl she had seen them in books, but she had grown doubtful of such things at an early age. It was hard to believe in magic when her own life didn't seem to have any sparkle.

The three girls were shown to a suite of ornate rooms. In the bedroom was a magnificent four poster bed. Nikki almost squealed with delight when she saw it and threw herself on top of it. Food was brought to them on silver trays and they were encouraged to ask for anything they liked. In the bathroom was a large bath with four golden feet, shaped like dogs' paws. Lucy began running steaming water into the bath immediately.

'Ellie?' Nikki said, from the bed.

Ellie was lying on a long couch, eating chocolate biscuits. 'Yes,' she replied, with a mouthful of crumbs.

'Thanks for rescuing me. You didn't have to. You could have left me in that dungeon and never had to see me again.'

Ellie swallowed her biscuit. 'No, we couldn't. Lucy was right. No one deserves to be left in the hands of Maleaver. And look at us now. We're friends, aren't we?'

'I hope so,' Nikki said. 'I'm sorry for being so horrible at school.'

Ellie shrugged. 'Maybe you had your reasons. But now you can be different.'

'I will,' Nikki said, earnestly. 'I promise.'

'Cool!' Ellie said, and went back to munching biscuits.

The party was every bit as good as the last fairy party Ellie and Lucy had been to. There were coloured lanterns around the garden, a fairy band, lots of dancing, plenty of delicious food and many fairies, all wanting to speak to them. Nikki was, once again, speechless, as fairies even wanted to talk to *her* and thank her. Acantha, Adalira and Fychan were surrounded all night by friends, eager to know about their adventures.

Gabriella was beautiful, in a shimmering turquoise dress. She greeted Lucy, Ellie and Nikki with a huge hug. 'Come on, I've got someone special who wants to see you,' she said, pulling Lucy and Ellie by the hands.

They both shrieked, in delight, as they saw Perizam wobbling towards them. Throwing their arms around him, they smothered the little man in kisses. He blushed from head to toe and on his face was a grin that spread from ear to ear. Lucy danced around him, excitedly telling him all that had happened. Ellie tried to calm her down and answer Perizam's questions more sensibly.

They introduced him to Nikki and he bowed his head graciously to her, which for some reason started tears flowing down her cheeks.

'Don't cry, Nikki,' Lucy said, finally coming to a halt. 'Everything's alright now.'

'I can't help it, ' Nikki said. 'I've never been happier.'

That night the three girls slept in the four poster bed together. It was so enormous there was plenty of room for them all. But the next morning they all felt the pull of home calling them.

'It's time we were leaving, isn't it,' Lucy said.

Ellie nodded, feeling the familiar tug between the two worlds.

After breakfast, they met with Queen Hermia, Prince Lysander and Gabriella.

'It's time for you to leave, isn't it?' Gabriella asked, sadly.

'Yes,' Ellie said.

'We will make sure you get there safely,' the Queen said. 'Adalira, Acantha and Fychan would like to escort you to the path in the woods. And, of course, Perizam is coming too.'

'Don't forget us,' Gabriella said.

'We never could, 'Ellie replied. 'And you know where to find us.'

The walk back to the magical path in the woods was full of chatter and laughter. When they reached the path it was hard to say the final goodbye.

'Take care, my little ones,' Perizam said, as Lucy and Ellie and Nikki headed down the path. Acantha, Adalira and Fychan stood waving, as the three girls suddenly disappeared from sight. The girls held tightly to each other as they whirled through the air, back to their own world. They landed, with a bump, back in the copse at school. Looking down at themselves, they saw that they were back in their school uniforms.

'I wonder what time it is,' said Lucy.

'Or even what day,' said Nikki.

Ellie suddenly had a moment of doubt, as she looked at Nikki Walters in her school uniform. 'Did you mean what you said back in Elysia, Nikki?'

'Every word,' Nikki said, solemnly.

'We need to keep this a secret,' Ellie said.

'Of course. We don't want everyone knowing that Ellie Deaver believes in fairies, do we?' Nikki grinned.

The bell rang, for end of lunch time, and they realised that no time at all had passed here.

Lucy put out her hand. Ellie put hers on top and pulled Nikki's on top of hers. 'Together. Whatever!' Lucy said.

'Together. Whatever!' Nikki and Ellie answered. And the three friends ran, laughing, out of the copse, and back to their own classrooms.